THE HOSAN

THE HOSANNA MAN

a novel by

Philip Callow

Foreword by

John Lucas

Shoestring  Press

Printed by imprintdigital
Upton Pyne, Exeter
www.imprintdigital.net

Typeset by types of light
typesoflight@gmail.com

Published by Shoestring Press
19 Devonshire Avenue, Beeston, Nottingham, NG9 1BS
(0115) 925 1827
www.shoestringpress.co.uk

First published: Jonathan Cape, 1956
This edition 2014
Copyright © The Estate of Philip Callow

The moral right of the author has been asserted

Author photograph by Pauline Lucas

ISBN 978 1 907356 87 2

FOREWORD

The Hosanna Man, Philp Callow's first novel, was published in 1956, when the author was thirty-two. It is set in Nottingham, to which Callow had moved from his native Coventry, partly because of a love affair and partly at the suggestion of Ray Gosling, whose early writings Callow admired, and who himself had recently taken up residence in the city. But Nottingham had the added attraction of being associated with D.H. Lawrence. It is easy now to be unaware of or to under-estimate the huge, almost magnetic influence Lawrence exercised on working-class writers and intellectuals in the first half of the last century. Callow was not merely inspired by Lawrence, he saw in him someone whose experiences both pre-figured his own and whose creative output – in novels, poetry, plays, essays, even in painting – provided the example he needed, gave him the confidence to believe in the worth, the validity, of his own creative impulses. Callow loved and admired other writers, but no-one mattered to him more than Lawrence. This is evident from a mere glance at the two-volume biography he would eventually write of him: *Son and Lover: The Young Lawrence*, and, later, *Body of Truth: D.H. Lawrence: The Nomadic Years, 1919–1930*.

For many, perhaps for most working-class writers, the influence of Lawrence was at best a mixed blessing. Cetainly, there are a goodly number of now-forgotten novels which in the 1940 and 50s were much praised because metropolitan reviewers thought, or anyway said, that they reproduced the authentic 'raw' voice of working class experience. Proletarian, kitchen-sink writing was for a time fashionable. Then the fashion changed and when it did the novels I have in mind vanished.

The Hosanna Man also vanished, – literally. In fact, soon after its publication, the novel was taken off the shelves of bookshops and libraries. Not, however, because it was no good. The explanation is altogether different. Jonathan Cape, who had published it and who by the time it came out already had Callow's second novel, *Common People*, ready for publication, pulped the one and cancelled their contract with the author for his second novel. The explanation – though certainly not justification – for this treatment of Callow was that a newsagent on Nottingham's Mansfield Road who claimed to detect a less than flattering, indeed libellous, reference to himself in *The Hosanna Man*, proposed to sue the author for libel. In those far-off days of the 1950s the sale of certain novels – all the way from John Cleland's eighteenth-century erotic fantasy *Fanny Hill* through to the unexpurgated *Lady Chatterley's Lover* – was forbidden by law. No surprise, then, that bookshops and newsagents made money by selling them 'under the counter.'

Callow did no more than hint at this particular newsagent's 'muckiness' but it was quite enough for the newsagent to see his chance to make a dishonest penny or two. A writ was issued. Cape advised Callow to settle out of court. Their lawyers suggested £300 would do the trick, and Callow, who by then had left Nottingham and was working as a naval clerk in Plymouth, was told he had no alternative but to pay out. The upshot was that he found himself penniless and without a publisher. Fortunately, Bodley Head took on *Common People*, no doubt encouraged by the number of hugely favourable reviews in the national press which – irony of ironies – were recommending *The Hosanna Man* to readers at the very time the novel itself was being pulped.

Though this blow shook Callow badly, it did not put a stop to his writing. He went on to publish a further fourteen novels, the last of which, *Black Rainbow*, was published by Shoestring Press (1999), as were three of his collections of poetry; the same press also published *Passage from Home* (2002), his account of his early years, and in the intensity of its writing one of his finest works. But he would never allow *The Hosanna Man* to be reprinted. 'Bad karma,' he said of a work which nearly ended his career before it properly began. And right up to his death in 2007 he could hardly bring himself to talk about it. Now, at last, Shoestring Press is privileged to re-publish a work which should never have been allowed to go out of print.

Readers coming to the novel for the first time will, I think, realise that despite the well-intended praise of some of his critics, Callow is no more a proletarian novelist than was Lawrence. His abiding love is for language, for what it can reveal of the psyche and how it can be recruited to testify to the vitality of emotions and the life of things. He has no great interest in narrative or plot, is largely indifferent to the 'well-made' novel; but his sensitivity to the deep, evocative power of words, his responsiveness to place and his subtle understanding of currents of feeling and their psychological import are, Lawrence always excepted, like no other writer. In some ways, though, especially in his scrupulous, unmoralising powers of observation, he is Chekhovian. He wrote a fine biography of the great Russian writer, as he did of the artists and poets he most admired, among them Blake, Van Gogh, Cézanne, and Walt Whitman. In his *History of Reading*, Alberto Manguel says that it was Callow's biography of the American poet that gave him 'a clearer picture of the man' than any of the more conventional, academic studies he had encountered.

Callow would have been pleased by such praise. And it is to be hoped that his shade will be appeased by the re-publication of the novel which once caused him such undeserved anguish.

We are very grateful to Anne Callow for making possible the publication of this edition, printed from the original text of 1956.

John Lucas

THE HOSANNA MAN

Chapter 1

I AM a Midlander, born in Birmingham, the only son of a Nuneaton girl. I don't remember my sister; she died when I was four. But my mother is very much alive. She is short and energetic, and always hurrying somewhere, holding herself rather grimly. She is still shy, though old age has sharpened her tongue a little.

My father enlisted under-age in the Gloucestershires, just after the outbreak of the First World War. Afterwards he had any number of jobs. He was an adventurous, independent person. I remember him telling me once about some of his jobs. He had been a railwayman, machinist, pawnbroker's clerk, milk roundsman, garage manager; and there were others I have forgotten. He is dead now. He was a tall, bony man, his thin body full of angles, charged with restlessness. His dark moustache seemed a sort of tradition in his family, passed on like a mark of obstinate virility. The upper lip was always left unshaven.

My mother has always told me that I am a fool, like my father. She means by this that I have inherited his restlessness. But I have changed a good deal during the past few years. I have a wife now, and two small daughters. There are moments where I simply sit down, doing nothing. I can see the long line of a hill through my window, and now and again I become absorbed in it. This kind of thing is happening to me for the first time. The roar of the world has grown less frightening, steadier, more like a pulse-beat. I can remember when a noise used to madden me, shrilling in my ears, full of petrol, brains, insanity.

At this very moment I am smoking a pipe. On fine evenings I dig in a garden. I have certainly changed. Perhaps it is only a temporary calmness, but it is like the advantage of high ground when you wish to survey your journey. I can look back, gaze down on a map of chance, and see decisive turnings. I can stand and ponder without distraction.

I had been wandering about the country for a time, trying to decide what to do with my life, struggling and then drifting with the tide. For a long while I had been obsessed by the fact of my isolation. Bits of life fell into me like stones into a pond, so that I was stirred without being able to move. I was always on the fringe, at the edge of things, the eternal spectator. Some conspiracy seemed to arrange everything so that I was kept suspended, walking parallel. I made violent efforts, trying to brutalize myself, goading myself to walk into the middle of activities where I didn't belong, taking blind steps and gulping down my fears. Yet nothing ever came of these efforts. The conspiracy leaned down and jerked me back, gasping with relief. Then I felt angry and ashamed, degraded, and somehow, worst of all, I felt less than a man. It was a foolish and unnecessary struggle, yet my desire was always simple and unshaken, regardless of every failure. I wanted to walk and walk until I vanished into life.

I had been in London. Then I came back for a fortnight's holiday with my mother, who lived in a cottage now, at Broadway in the Cotswolds. I kept toying all the time I was there with some vague idea I had of emigrating to Canada or Australia. But I wasn't sure. It seemed such an abstract idea, too blind a step even for me. And there was Stella. It was no use making any plans, I realized, until I had ended what I had begun with her.

There was her last letter to me, the last I ever received. It was a fantastic affair, made absurd with theatrical nonsense about her husband's growing jealousy, his hints and suspicions. She wrote that the whole atmosphere at her home had thrown her into an 'agony of fear and remorse', not for fear of herself, but she dreaded the thought of hurting him again, for 'the second time'. I didn't remember any mention of this being a second time, and I tried to recall all her letters, to remember if she had ever referred to it before. Was it an invention, something to add to the blaze? She went on to say that the first time, when he had found out, she had nearly gone insane because it almost 'broke him'. She was going slowly mad in the poisonous atmosphere, she repeated; little by little every one of her fears were being confirmed, and now she was *certain* that he knew everything and was playing a fiendish cat-and-mouse game with her. How wretched it all was, and she was so sick with remorse that she could 'lie down in the river'. I smiled icily at this touch of Ophelia, reading on, reading every word. She loved her husband, really loved him, worthless as she was – did I understand? Was I capable of understanding that she really loved only him, and could not bear to hurt him? And she had ended this gay letter, all written firmly and clearly in bright green ink, by announcing that she could not go on; she felt foul, abominable, rotten

5

to the core. In her very last sentence she begged me to stop writing to her, in a way which read like an order.

Then there was a long postscript, written hastily, the lines sloping down to one side, concerning her friend Connie. This Connie she had trusted implicitly as her one real friend. She had often spoken of her with warm affection. For a while I had been sending my letters to Connie's house, for Stella to collect; and this had been Stella's own idea. Now she was certain that Connie had begun an affair with her husband and was showing my letters to him, somehow unsealing them without it being apparent. 'Oh, how it sickens me, this treachery, this betrayal,' wrote Stella in the postscript. 'It all disgusts me, everything. The way I feel at this moment, I could kill myself . . .' and so on. It was characteristic of her, the phrase 'at this moment'. No doubt the moment would pass, the whole set of circumstances dissolve with bewildering swiftness, and then how would she feel? I took her letter seriously, but I knew how susceptible she was to outward things, even a slight movement of furniture disturbing her, or a certain odour. She built up emotions and tensions and let them founder with lightning rapidity. If I accused her of wavering and uncertainty, as I often did when we were together, she only said, 'Don't depend on me. I'm rotten, I'm hell to live with. Do you know,' smiling, 'I even shock myself! I weep out of one eye, and at the same instant I'm winking with the other.' Or if she felt she had a tragic role to play, she would say, making her face mask-like, 'I'm evil – I can't help it. I'll always be like that. It's how I'm made.'

Her letters always left me angry or irritable, even when

6

they were pleasant ones. It could have been that ink. It had an acid look. Something happened to her in her letters, taking possession of her. There is a dangerous freedom about an empty page, a white sheet of paper; and a pen has a sharp point. She always said that she enjoyed writing letters. I believed her. The bad ones left me each time with an intense feeling of impotence, obscure humiliation, and out of this rose a desire, quite murderous, for revenge, a lustful, sensual thing. I became full of poisonous juice which pressed behind my eyes, deforming the world. It became torment to me to be so far away when I felt that the only way to regain my self-respect was to inflict some pain on her, a scathing remark, a cruel, unanswerable question – anything. A kind of nervous love-hate took possession of me, of extraordinary power, making me tremble all over. I had read descriptions of the awful passion of jealousy, without experiencing it myself; now it seemed to fit my condition perfectly, as I sat wherever I happened to be, with one of those letters in my hand. It was as if my will had been sucked out of me. I knew I no longer had control of myself. I had no balance, no humour. I could feel myself toppling into a black horrible place.

Our correspondence came to an abrupt end with this last letter of hers, simply because I could no longer reply. It was forbidden to write to her house or to Connie's. It seemed incredible that Connie had really betrayed us, yet in her letter Stella hinted at 'absolute proof'. She gave me only one concrete example. Her husband had actually used a phrase out of one of my letters, one night as they were going to bed, letting it drop casually. It had made her blood freeze. She had waited for the flood of accusations, but none came. I read this part two or three times, unable to believe it. It was an amazing, fiendish situation, if it was true. I had never seen this Connie. All I knew of her, was that she had black hair, smoothed straight with oil and knotted at the back. I kept thinking of this black, slippery hair.

I could think of no way around the problem, yet I refused to accept this as the end of our affair. How could anything end so wretchedly, so inconclusively? It peered out from my other failures with a face of such derision that I refused to accept its reality. And I was seething with answers, with questions, with words to attack her with. I kept writhing under the oblique humiliation of it all, even though she protested that she blamed only herself. That was her pride. Yet it was not, it was her pride perverted. How dare she drag our affair into such common mud? How dare she want to 'beg forgiveness' of her husband? I shaped and hammered these rhetorical questions like knives, like weapons, as though she were there before me. How dare she drag me with her into that mess of remorse? Wasn't that just much a cause for shame, to feel foul because of her affair with me? With all my might I was trying to salvage the remains of my own pride and vanity.

I could not write any of this to her, to rid myself of it. It gathered me in me like a poison. How could I even go to see her now and speak to her, when it was impossible to write and arrange a meeting-place? In my mind I thrashed about for days, unable to think of anything. For a long time I had hated the everlasting secrecy, the intrigue. Stella had said to me quite honestly, 'I love an intrigue.' She had said it with relish. I admired her, but I could never agree with her. I was the dishonest one, not her, because of my youth and idealism.

In the mornings, lying in bed listening to my mother moving below, I would sniff at the air. The little window, no more than a foot square, would be slightly open, and almost at my elbow. I could smell the winter; it was still lodged firmly in the fields and trees. But there was something else. It came through the window, softly, running straight into my veins. And I had a sudden idea. Why couldn't I simply go to her city, just arrive, and hang around there outside her house until she came out? It seemed so obvious a solution that I couldn't understand my stupidity. Really it had not been stupidity before, but lack of courage.

Then a better idea came. I would go to the school where she met her daughter each week-day in order to bring her across the main road. I would plant myself there, on the doorstep, and wait. By meeting her there I should be away from the house. It was a magnificent idea, bound to succeed. I didn't know the school by name, yet I swept this difficulty aside as trivial. All I had to do was to find the school nearest to her home, the nearest primary school. Picturing this meeting in my imagination, I faltered; it seemed so preposterous all at once. How would she react, I asked myself, coming suddenly face to face with me in the street, when she had thought I was at the other end of the country? But I had to risk that. I had nothing whatever to lose. Even if she refused to speak to me, I should be in no worse a position than I was now. The more

I thought about it, brooded over it, the more ridiculously easy it seemed, though I took care not to let any thoughts of the actual meeting enter my mind. I imagined it as already accomplished. I decided to find lodgings in Nottingham as soon as I arrived, and later on I would have to get work of some kind. It didn't matter to me; I told myself that I might as well be there as anywhere else.

Chapter 2

A T the end of my second week we had a visitor. It was Harry, an uncle of mine. He was my father's only brother. The same dark moustache shadowed his lip; he was thin, but not so tall, and about six years younger than my father. I had not seen him for a long time. I kept following the movements of his long, bony hands, work-reddened, and listening to the sound of his voice. His head was curiously flat on the top, and his face had a hungry look, like a man who had not had his full share of life. Certainly he was a hungry, indiscriminate reader. Whenever his eyes saw print his long hands reached out, no matter what it was.

He had come for the week-end, and was driving back to Coventry in his car on Easter Monday. So I decided to go back with him, then travel by bus from there to Nottingham. When I told him what my destination was, he gave me a startled look.

'Why Nottingham?' he said.

I wasn't surprised by this question, but he asked it in such a friendly, human way that I felt ashamed at having to deceive him. 'Oh, I don't know, really. I just thought I'd like to live there for a time. I've got a few friends there'.

It was a lie; apart from Stella, I didn't know anyone. All at once it seemed the most ridiculous thing I had ever done. I tightened my lips.

I thought Harry was about to question me further. Probably he was, and something in my face prevented him. His eyes looked curious, then faintly bewildered, and then the light of interest died out in them. He went on reading out of some book I had left on one of the chairs. He was naturally a silent man; I had always liked him for that. Sitting there awkwardly in his best clothes, his blue serge suit and white shirt, he looked every inch a working-man with time on his hands. He sat uneasily, almost like a youth, awkward about his hands and feet, though he was past middle-age. His long, secret face, with slow eyes, still had a boyish look, and around his mouth there was a sadness, the mark of his defeat and resignation. I always vowed that my face would never wear that look. He had pulled up all his drawbridges, he was firmly entrenched in his own world where nothing could disturb him, snug behind his layers of shyness. It would have been so easy for me to become like that. I knew better than to confide in him.

On Monday morning I sat in the front seat of his car, parked in the empty lane outside the cottage. We were about half a mile from the village. My suitcase was on the back seat, bound together with a black webbing strap.

'Good-bye, Louis,' my mother said softly, through the car window. I don't think she had meant to do that. It was an impulse at the last minute. She retreated into the cottage and shut the door quickly, before we moved off. Then I glimpsed her face at the leaded window for an instant, as we drove away.

I began to breathe more freely, to feel happy and excited. We didn't speak a word for the first twenty miles or so. I had known Harry for a long time, since early boyhood. I had been camping with him many a summer. Now we sat together, two men, moving swiftly through the countryside. I watched his hands move, tightening and relaxing on the controls, vibrating on the wheel or the gear-leaver, the engine throbbing up through them. His hands had calm, contained movements. He had a strange way of urging the car forward if he had to pass anyone or climb a steep hill, pressing himself forward on the wheel, rocking to and fro slightly in his seat. He was unconscious of what he did. I was giving him occasional sidelong glances, and I suddenly realized what a gentle man he was. As the car sped on, nosing carefully through the towns, slackening speed as we entered villages, I felt no desire to speak. I thought of us, gliding effortlessly across these fields and hills; two men. One young, one old. I kept wondering about Harry's life, which struck me as being a very lonely one. But nothing would have made me ask him about it. I respected his silence. I knew only the bare bones, the outlines of his life; no more than that. He was a skilled machinist in the printing trade, and he had never married. He lived in Coventry with an unmarried sister.

Suddenly he turned to me, a cheerful grin lighting up his face. 'Won't be long now.'

'No,' I said.

Then he said: 'Shall we stop somewhere and have a drink somewhere?'

I told him I wouldn't mind.

We got out at a pub called The Hand of Friendship, on the main road at the outskirts of a small town. Harry asked me to get the drinks, as I knew he would, putting a pound note in my hand.

'I'll be in here,' he said, and went into a small, bare, stone-flagged room.

As we sat with our beer, and I was looking round at the queer shape of the room, he blurted out, 'How are you off for money?' He wrinkled his face painfully, to disguise his embarrassment. I think he would have been relieved if I had asked him for some. I told him that I had enough to last for about a month, but that I expected to get a job before then.

He sipped his beer, perching forward on the hard bench.

'What sort of job?' he said in a colourless voice.

'Oh, a clerk, I expect. I'll have to see.'

And he looked up shrewdly.

'What's the money like?' he asked. 'Does a clerk get much these days?'

Money was common ground for us both, and bridged the gulf a little between us. I think that was what he wanted. I told him the wages varied according to the responsibility, though it was never a great deal. I was grateful when he dropped the subject; his voice had gone flinty and unnatural.

The room was pleasantly bare. There was nothing but our small table, with the two benches, probably because it had only just been whitewashed. Being so empty, it was possible to enjoy to the full the unusual lopsided shape of the floor, the walls sloping inwards, narrowing together at the fireplace end. Three black beams, the wood gouged and split, ancient, made the ceiling massive over our heads.

We got back into the car and drove on, once more in

silence. When I think of it now, it seems strange. We are always like that when we are together. We come from the same class, the same city. We are like brothers, despite our difference of age; unspeaking, with sometimes a powerful hostility rising up between us, that leaves us with stronger bonds than ever when it dies, as it does with brothers. We respect each other's secrets. With some people I am tongue-tied. Sitting with Harry I fall silent, naturally.

We were in the suburbs of Coventry now, driving past all kinds of milestones in my life, as if reviewing them. Since my mother had left, three years ago, I had not revisited the place. The car ran on swiftly, driving in heedlessly, past my old school, then another school, then the factory where I had served an apprenticeship. Even the hospital where my grandfather had died after the street accident. And of course there countless other things, small things, each one giving its tiny sign. Yet none of it mattered now. I had escaped. I was only visiting, passing through; I had no connection with it. Because of this, perhaps, it was somehow ghastly now, a place of ghosts. I could hardly wait to get on the Leicester bus.

Harry drove me into the bus station at Pool Meadow. He switched off the engine, and there was a last faint shudder into silence. Everything seemed unnaturally quiet. I had to jerk myself to life. As I dragged out my suitcase and dumped it on the pavement, Harry sat quite absently, as if in a trance, gazing through his smeared windscreen.

'Everything all right?' he muttered in a far-away voice, not looking at me.

'Yes, thanks. Thanks very much for the lift.' I was about

15

to turn, lifting up the case, when he suddenly came to life.

'Yes, yes, all right – everything all right? You sure? Cheerio, then, Lou – Look after yourself.'

I tried not to look at his face. I guessed that even a second's silence was painful to him at this moment.

'I'll say cheerio, then!' he cried again, and even as he spoke he was working furiously at the controls, saying something over his shoulder to me, but before I could speak again the car was curving round and driving away.

A bunch of drivers and conductors were standing a few yards away. They all stood with their hands in their pockets, and they had that slightly contemptuous, arrogant air of men who have had a surfeit of travel, of people incessantly coming and going. They had stared too long at the futility of it to be unaffected. They might have been removal men, transporters of homes, instead of people. They had that same air of vacancy and arrogance, as if nothing could move without them, and they had seen so much of it.

I went up to the nearest one, a burly, white-haired man, to ask the time of the next Leicester bus.

'What bus?'

'Leicester.'

The broad-shouldered driver surveyed the scene. As he looked, a bus swung into sight, approaching us, pulling up about ten yards away. It began to empty out its passengers.

'Get on that,' said the driver, and turned away.

The sky had gone grey. There was a slight drizzle falling. The buildings, squatting about as if dejected, were all of a grim, soot-encrusted red brick, looking as if charred by fire.

It all chilled me, hollowing me out, but when I shivered it was half excitement. I was the first to board the bus. I sat near the back, watching each new passenger. Then the driver clambered back into his cabin, and I saw his hand feel for the starter.

Before we had travelled very far, I began to feel sick in the stomach. It was all the travelling I had done that day, all by road. I felt myself turning pale, my hands growing cold.

I sat huddled in my seat, looking out miserably at the procession of allotments and hen-coops, the corrugated-iron sheds, front gardens, railway lines, rusty gasometers, cemeteries. None of it had changed, yet it all looked uglier than I had ever seen it. We reached Leicester, running swiftly in among the flat, long streets, and at the terminus I stumbled out, gulping down fresh air.

Opposite the entrance to the terminus there was a café, a squalid-looking place. I went in there for a cup of tea. It was even more sordid inside than out. I hardly noticed who else was there; my limbs were paining me, and my face felt grey. Sipping the hot drink, I found myself smiling round like an imbecile, without knowing why. I was in a queer state. Somebody behind me said: 'Lousy weather, ain't it?' and touched my shoulder.

'Rotten,' I said, turning in my seat to see who had spoken. It was a labourer I had known at the factory in Coventry, when I had worked there. He was grinning like a demon. 'How's Lou?' he mouthed out of his grin, in his hoarse voice. He turned to a crony and started to tell him how long it was since he had seen me.

17

His hair was greased flat on his head, eaten away at the temples like a mouldy fur. The skin of his face was so bloodless it looked evil, startlingly white, and somehow soiled and sordid. His mouth was broad and shapeless, with hardly any lips. He had always gone out of his way to be friendly to me; I never knew why.

'Off to the races, me,' he said, winking. 'Beer and races, today; beer and races, that's life!'

I had a few words with him, then made an excuse and went outside. There was a green bus standing in the terminus, leaving for Nottingham in half an hour, so I got in and sat down. My sickness had begun to go away now. This coach had deep, soft, luxurious seats, the last word in comfort. As I sank into mine I felt like an invalid. Within five minutes all the bones in my body were aching pleasurably. Gradually the coach filled up, and as we moved off a radio began to give out music, falteringly. Once more I was near the back, and had a view of about twenty heads. A fat, red-faced conductor was moving slowly up the centre towards me. All at once everything made me want to laugh out loud – the hidden radio, the passengers in front of me, sunk out of sight and only their heads showing, the fat, ministering conductor and even the pompous majesty of the bus as it rolled along. We were all helpless with comfort. I wondered if anyone else realized how comical we must have looked. I gave my companion a quick glance. His beefy face was blank and expressionless as he studied his paper; I doubt if he even knew we were out of Leicester.

We were on a broad, gritty, curving road, slipping through

open country, the sun shining. I kept thinking of Stella, of the expression on her face, of the reception I would get. It was all an unknown quantity, all of it. Anything could happen. The palms of my hands were damp because of my excitement, and, I suppose, my fears. New meetings are always an ordeal to me. The bus was jolting forward slowly over a rough road, going through a village, and I saw a bed-and-breakfast sign. It gave me a little shock, reminding me that I should have to find somewhere cheap to stay when I arrived. The cheaper the place, the longer I could delay starting another job. I thought this in less than second, after noticing the sign – and then the desire rose up to me, paradoxically, to get a job, not to delay at all, and to start work as soon as possible. For three months I had done nothing; it was my longest period of idleness since I had left school. I had been following a vague, stubborn conviction which had slowly formed itself into an out-and-out refusal to do anything but my real work. But it was difficult to be certain what that was. Sitting in the bus, I reasoned that I was too unsettled in myself to attempt any creative activity, and now, as I thought of it, the aimlessness of my life sickened me. I felt slack and unhealthy. In my queer, distracted state I needed some routine work for a while, so that I could pull myself together. In my real self I wanted to remain shapeless and undecided for a while, though it would have been hard to say why. It was perhaps a natural instinct to turn to work at this time of darkness and confusion, a simple remedy for misery. And I had never been idle. I had always been dogged to apply myself to some task.

Chapter 3

Now we were pulling into Nottingham, crossing the River Trent at West Bridgford, and I looked out curiously at these streets that I hardly knew at all, my thoughts swinging back to Stella. I had been here once as a youth, with some apprentices from the factory, to see the Australians at Trent Bridge. And more recently I had been here on two week-end trips to see Stella, about eight or nine months ago. That was all. It was so alien and looked so vast, a world to itself, in which I had no part, no real business, that I had a moment of icy terror, gazing out, my spine going suddenly cold. The bus glided in, smoothly penetrating the tangle of streets, past huge sooty factories, garages, shops, a railway station, the Labour Exchange, then a bus depot, a vast cavernous place full of trolley buses, looming red monsters in the shadows. Three or four drivers stood outside, one of them leaning back against the scarred wall. Then we swung into the bus station, alongside the new vegetable market.

My first thought was to try the Y.M.C.A., since I had just become a member. I went straight to the new brick building in Shakespeare Street. It was one of the few places I knew.

They had no more accommodation.

'We're full up,' said the clerk at the desk. 'You can try Shakespeare Villas if you like, just down the street. They usually take our overflows. Here, have this,' and he gave me a soiled piece of card, with the address printed in pencil, in large, shaky letters.

'Thanks,' I said, turning away in confusion to look at the card. I had not expected this. After his first words I had not really understood what he had said. When I turned back to ask for directions he was talking rapidly to a young girl. They were laughing together, and then the girl looked curiously at me. I walked outside and started walking downhill.

I came to a side street, with a block of Council Offices occupying one corner. It was Shakespeare Villas. The house I wanted was at the end, almost at the cul-de-sac. The narrow street had about fifteen dingy houses on either side, each house with its derelict scrap of garden in front. The blind end of the street was completely sealed by some sort of factory shed, a big single-storey construction. I could see a pulley with a segment missing, revolving on its shaft through a square hole near the roof, and with each revolution something clanked, not very loud, like clockwork. The street was absolutely quiet and deserted as I walked up it with my suitcase; there was just this dull, heaving tocking from the turning shaft.

I stood at the door, only a few houses from the factory. This garden was as forsaken as a desert, its grimy hedge full of dead branches. The knocker had jammed, I was unable to move it, so I knocked with my fist as hard as I could, hearing echoes inside, as if the place was empty. There was a shuffling sound and then the door opened.

An old, heavy man stood there, with a massive belly, his filthy waistcoat half-unbuttoned and the corners curling up. His eyes were humorous and wide-awake, under the cloth cap he wore. He had an old-fashioned dense moustache, untrimmed, stained by tobacco, the kind I remember seeing on my grandfather's face when he had been a railway guard.

He stood leaning up against the doorpost, waiting for me to speak. I told him that I was looking for lodgings.

'You'd better come in, lad,' he said roughly, in strong Nottinghamshire, 'and talk to the missus.'

I followed him down the passage as he shuffled along, supporting himself on the wall with one hand. We entered a small, high room, with a window looking onto a narrow, cobbled yard, hemmed in on all sides.

There was an old iron range which had a bright blazing fire in it. I could hear sounds of running water from a kitchen, but the old man looked straight at the door we had just come through as he stood propped against the table, his little round head sunk down on his large body, between his sloping shoulders.

'Missus!' he bellowed, making me jump. 'You're wanted, Missus!'

Then he moved a few inches and sat down very slowly in an enormous old leather armchair under the window, and picked up his pipe.

'Sit down, boy,' he mumbled, filling his pipe. He waved an arm at me, grandly, as though the room was full of furniture. But it was incredibly bare and poverty-stricken. The only thing of comfort in it was the fire, which was well stoked up. The window was half-covered by a strip of coarse yellow canvas which had been nailed to the frame, so that when you sat down you were unable to see out. Apart from a wooden kitchen chair at the table, there was only a narrow, half-broken leather sofa against the wall. It was all cracks and bulges. I sat on that, gingerly.

'Missus!' roared the old man, staring directly at me. With his left hand he held his empty pipe, sucking at it noisily, and the other hand rested across his full stomach, which swelled out abruptly. It looked as if he were holding it back, or nursing a parcel, like something that had nothing to do with his body. I was fascinated by this great belly of his.

The door to the kitchen opened and his wife came out. She was small and quick, with large, badly-swollen hands, and seemed a good deal younger than her husband.

'Oh!' she said, stopping suddenly; and she became very formal. 'Good evenin', young man.' Although she was bent, she moved with surprising swiftness. She had darted round the table and was dragging the kitchen chair out to face the fire, crying out at the same time, 'You'll be cold there; don't sit there, love – draughty, nasty – will you sit here? Yes, yes, of course you will. Won't he, Mister? He will – yes, of course he will!' She chattered on at a tremendous rate, jerking her head from her husband to me and back again, talking about me in the third person, as if I were not there. Her old eyes burned in her face.

I went and sat in the chair like an obedient schoolboy.

'Thank you very much.'

'That's better, course it is – eh, Mister? No charge for that, no charge; have a nice warm – now then!' She stood at my back, her hands resting on the chair a moment. 'Would you like a cup of tea, young man? A hot cup of tea? What about you, Mister? – no need to ask you. Yes, of course you would;

cup of tea, both of you; all right.' She had disappeared into the kitchen again before I could speak.

We sat there in a weird silence, the old man not offering to speak. I was gazing fixedly into the fire, a bit at a loss.

'We've just got the pension, we only have that comin' in. That's why we put folks up. Pension's not much these days,' the old man said deliberately, as though I had asked him something.

'No, that's right,' I said. 'It's nothing now.'

'Been retired five years. Used to be at pit-top. You know a pit?'

'Well, yes, in a way,' I said, grinning at him stupidly, not quite understanding.

'You know the engine that pulls up cage?' he persisted, sitting lumpy and inert, only his eyes alive.

'Oh yes.'

'I used to look after it,' he stated, with a heavy pride. 'That's what my job was. Not far from here, where I worked – was it, Missus?' he suddenly said in a louder voice, still looking straight at my face. 'Don't do nothing now, though. Did forty years at it. Finished now.'

'Just gets fat now, sits and gets fat – eh, Mister?' his wife chimed in, bringing in the tea. She put the tray on the table. 'Now then, let's give this young man something to drink; never mind the pit. Not interested in pits, are you – no, course not!'

'Nor in your chatter, he's not,' muttered the old man brutally, lurching suddenly to his feet. I gazed in awe at his massive bulk. He shambled across the room, moving with

24

difficulty, clutching at furniture for support.

'Now what are you after? Can't sit still, can't rest,' cried his wife irritably at his broad back. 'He's gone for the paper!' she hissed at me furiously, bending down at my side. Her hands were twitching and pinching like claws with irritation. I could hear him shuffling down the passage, on the return journey. 'Bad on his feet, but he must have his paper, must get it himself – silly old man.'

'Sit down, sit down, have your tea!' she cried at him, twitching her hands in her apron. He stood in the doorway.

'Shut up,' he mumbled, lurching past her with his paper.

Finally I managed to tell them what I really wanted. They looked at each other doubtfully when I said I should like full board. Apparently they only took in a few people for bed-and-breakfast, mainly at week-ends, to eke out the pension.

'You see, I'm old; I can't do a lot,' the old woman said, a shrewd little smile flitting on and off her face. She seemed made up of hundreds of nervous movements. She was never still. 'We're old,' she said. 'We don't like to bother much; we get tired.'

I explained that all I really wanted was bed and breakfast; I could buy my other meals out.

'We'll see, in a day or two,' was all she would say. 'See how you like it. You may not like it; never know. Now then – what about another cup of tea? Give me that cup, young man.'

I left it at that. It was almost eight. I went out into the streets for a walk, to look around. It was too late to think of meeting Stella – I would have to wait until Tuesday. In a way

I was relieved. I was too tired for emotions.

Without my suitcase I felt as light as a feather, frail and insubstantial. I walked close to the walls, as if a sudden gust of wind would blow me under a car. Wandering through the strange streets, knowing no one, I felt utterly blank and without individuality, nothing, as though I had no past, no home, no parents and no friends. It would have been easy to get lost, so I kept near the city centre, among the shops and traffic and theatre crowds.

I tried to realize that I had come here to live, but found it hard to grasp. Everything was unreal. Tomorrow I would make an attempt to meet Stella and also inquire at the labour exchange about a job.

I had no feelings of revenge or anger against her now. That had all died. I suddenly wanted to meet her now, in the softness of this night, in this strange city. Hadn't she said that she believed in me? Hadn't my poems brought tears to her eyes? I became full of impatience to meet her, and found myself walking very fast, back to my lodgings. There was power in me, I felt full to bursting with it, and I looked up at the dark sky. What was waiting, what was in store for me here? I revelled in the veil of mystery which shrouded everything, and forgot all the ugliness.

I was crossing Slab Square, a big open space flanked by shops and cinemas, the grandiose town hall at one end of it, with its stone lions and great round pillars. It reminded me a little of Trafalgar Square in London. I stopped for a few minutes to listen to the ranting of one of the local political speakers. He soon bored me, but I was interested in his audience. There was a little nucleus of resentment, so I stopped to see what would happen.

Standing behind the small crowd, I saw a woman whose features reminded me of Stella's. It was not a strong enough resemblance, but enough to send the flow of my thoughts in her direction once more; so I gave myself up to it, whirling back swiftly along a powerful river of memories.

I had first written to her three years ago from Coventry, when I was still living at home and working at the factory. Noticing one of her paintings in a local art exhibition there, I had got hold of her address and written a note expressing my admiration. Of course there was more than just admiration behind my action. I was terribly serious in those days, always in a desperate hurry and constantly bothered by my mortality. My youth never left me alone. I could hear the years running out under my feet like a tide, my skin drying with age, my mouth narrowing and tightening, my youth turning into skin and bones. The seas of life would dry up, shrink away, I thought, leaving me like a pebble that has never been moistened. I was haunted by this fear of a joyless life. It was a foolish state, but very real. My miserable experiences with girls, trying to strike up relationships with them, and all the pathetic and comic fruits I had tasted, left me with my mouth bitter. I lost faith in myself and what I sought. I became convinced that there was something queer about me. What was it? I was so hopelessly ill at ease and self-conscious when I was with girls. As soon as I could I got away from them and breathed a huge sigh of relief. But I knew that sooner or later I must have a wife, or a mistress – a woman of some kind. The moral aspect didn't really concern me. I wanted a wife and children, for I was convinced by this time that only something as radical as that could make a man of me, put an end to my restlessness. Perhaps then I could get down to some real work. I had decided that on my own I was far too proud, too gloomy. My egotism ate into me like an acid. Therefore I was looking for a wife. And I was naturally attracted to artists and what they stood for, broadly speaking; their love of freedom and truth, and their tolerance. I told myself, being young and full of hope: what could be better than an artist wife?

These ideas and conclusions were only shadows in my mind, I suppose, when I wrote the note, but they were there. I thought of it afterwards in amazement, when I fully realized my motives, and understood it for the thoroughly modern action it was. Without even seeing this woman or hearing her voice, I had arrived at the *idea* of it, an artist wife. . . .

Her reply came by return post, in the famous green ink. She nearly always wrote back immediately, unless she happened to be in the throes of an emotional crisis with her husband, or her child had fallen ill. Being an egotist, a super-egotist, as an artist always is, she revelled in letter-writing. She loved it, creating those little dramas and posting them off, regardless of the havoc they might cause at the other end. Stage manager, producer, leading star, whole company – Stella! I was addicted to it, too. Only I had pangs of shame, and at these moments I tried not to think of all the emotions I had blurted out on paper. This time I met my match. And she cured me.

From the beginning of our correspondence we flew at each other's throats. She wrote in such a provocative way, inviting attack. Yet she was perfectly sincere. I went off to London just after this first note, continuing the battle from there. She had told me at the beginning that she was married, and I was quick to observe the tinge of scorn, the challenge. It was a sort of spice. And in one sense it was because she was married that she had begun this thing with such energy. It provided a marvellous outlet for her discontent. She hated the thought of being merely a wife, a woman about the house. She could not forget her talents, and the thought of them going to waste tormented her. Her heart lay in all this resentment, cold and dangerous, ready to strike out in an instant.

Our letters became filled with artistic stuff, dogmatic statements on painting and poetry, abstract squabbles that served to disguise our passions. Before very long I grew impatient, and to pep things up, used to insert such phrases as 'if you don't stop writing such rubbish to me, I'll come up there and throttle you,' when I didn't agree with her. I wrote them at first out of genuine exasperation, angered by her arrogance. When I understood that she enjoyed them immensely, replying with even greater gusto, I repeated them often. There were all sorts of variations of this threat, and as a woman I suppose she appreciated their physical suggestiveness. Her responses now encouraged me to be more frank, bolder and more provocative. And her curiosity was thoroughly aroused; she wanted to know details of my appearance, how tall I was, and how old. And I glowed with satisfaction, marking this down as a real victory. Our letters were still full of ideas and discussions on general subjects, but they became more human, warm, and even humorous at moments.

She was a strange woman, unusually frank and free from prejudice, very tolerant, and able to derive the maximum enjoyment from a situation such as ours. I envied her. If I could have been as direct and honest as her, accepting it for what it was, I should have saved myself much misery. But I always wanted it to be something else. It was too obvious. I wanted it to take on mystery and depth, uniqueness. Underneath my modern skin I think I was also offended in my morals. If it had been utterly different from the affairs which other people had I would not have thought it sordid. I was not worldly enough. And knew hardly anything. Maupassant would have helped me a great deal, though I doubt if I would have given him a hearing; he would have been altogether too cynical for me. I did not even know that a woman can be sincere and insincere at one and the same time; and I attached far too much importance to words which fell out of people's mouths, or from the ends of their pens.

I think it was Stella's unshakeable belief that life would be unbearable without Art – by which she meant a sort of abstracted beauty – which repelled me most. I tried heaping abuse on her idols, exaggerating their human failings as maliciously as I could. Our battles mainly raged around this one focal point. I told her that her religion was really an insult to life, and once, in a fit of real anger, I wrote, 'I don't believe you when you say you love life; I don't think you care about anything that you can't make fixed and stunted and abstract inside a frame.' But nothing I did ever budged her from her faith.

Before very long she wanted to meet me. I wanted to meet her, of course, but I had an ordeal to face, with my dread of meeting strangers. I kept making excuses and cursing myself, trying to screw up courage. I would agree to her arrangements, then at the last minute lose my nerve and make another excuse. The very thought of such an encounter made me writhe. Stella evidently had no such nervousness, simply saying, 'I want to meet you. I'm curious. Where? When?' and underlining it firmly. I admired her always for that, making no bones about a thing; brushing aside the obstacles and plunging straight for whatever she wanted.

It was getting dark now. I stood behind the little crowd while the speaker rattled on endlessly. Someone at the front was goading him, but the man refused to lose his temper. 'You wait your turn,' he repeated every few minutes, in a loud, contained voice. 'When I've finished, you come up here and say your piece. You wait your turn matey.' He looked down coldly at the crowd out of an insolent, righteous face, as if they were all responsible for this solitary heckled. He tried to pick up the threads of his argument, but the man interrupted again. He sounded drunk.

'Listen,' the speaker barked. 'I don't know who you are, or who sent you. Who are you? What's your name? Come up here, come on. Say your piece up here.' He paused dramatically after this challenge. 'What you afraid of, brother?' he called

31

in an ugly voice.

There was no response. I was unable to see the heckler. The little crowd was hushed, waiting, all pressed forward. But the interrupter didn't speak. There was a long silence; somebody laughed. Nobody seemed to know what to do. The speaker stood obstinately silent and contemptuous, his arms folded, awaiting developments. I walked away. After I had gone a few yards some sort of commotion started up suddenly, with hoots of derisive laughter and somebody shouting, but I didn't stop. It was getting late. I walked back quickly through the dark streets, which seemed now very big and unknown, and streaming with people.

Chapter 4

THERE was not much sleep for me that night. I lay in
bed, in a single wooden bed near the door, trying to
get used to my surroundings. My body ached, and
at the bottom of my spine I could feel a steady gnawing pain,
but I felt wide awake.

It was a wretched room. A double bed, an ancient brass
affair, stood in the centre, high off the floor. It looked foolish,
like an exhibit, full of importance. And there were two other
single beds, against the walls. I had intended to read, but
the light was so dim and mournful that I had switched it
off, preferring the darkness. I noticed the strip of yellowish
canvas tacked over the lower part of the window, an exact
replica of the one downstairs. Above this a great sinister crack
zigzagged across one of the windowpanes, and in a top corner
there was a big triangle of glass missing. I could see all this by
the gas-light shining in drearily from the street. And outside
the pulley-shaft still revolved and ticked. Apparently it never
stopped.

I lay back luxuriously, glad in spite of everything. Then
I had a moment of panic. Would Stella resent me arriving
like this, after what she had said? Had she really finished
with me, after all? I thought suddenly that only an imbecile
would follow her and present himself as though nothing had
happened, after a letter like that. I struggled within myself,
feeling that my position was abject and degraded. What could
I do if she refused to speak? I no longer felt self-sufficient
and coolly exultant. The thought of all the swarming life

33

of this city, all alien, indifferent, made the possibility of a rebuff seem all at once monstrous. Before I had shrugged it off, thinking the outcome could not possibly harm me. That was before I had walked through the streets.

Was I in love with her? In my sensible moments I saw clearly enough that I had begun the whole thing, invented it and set it in motion, quite calmly and deliberately. Yet I believe that if I could have kept it on paper, the romance, I would have done it gladly, if only I could have quietened my own scorn. And her way of writing filled my head with wild thoughts. When she told me that she was coming on a visit to her mother's house in Coventry, and asked me to meet her there, I told her I would come.

On the morning of our meeting I cycled across the city to her mother's district, about a mile and a half from my home. Something churned inside me, I felt all hollowed out, and had to force my legs round. I found the house, far too quickly, and circled it slowly through the surrounding streets. I did this three or four times in an agony of mind, trying to make myself either ride away or go up to the door. When I finally knocked on the door it was opened by Stella's mother, who told me that Stella hadn't yet arrived. She said, 'She hasn't come back yet,' and had ushered me into the front room before I realized what she had said and began to puzzle over it. In actual fact Stella had already been to the house, but had gone out shopping.

'Would you like something to read?' her mother said, very formally, and gave me the morning newspaper. Then she went out of the room.

I felt a rush of gladness at having achieved this much. I was tremendously grateful for the chance to compose myself and try to appear at ease. The remembrance of all those mad letters of mine, in which I had practically pranced naked before her, made me tongue-tied with embarrassment now that I was about to meet her face to face. I glared around wildly, hoping even now for some avenue of escape, feeling the moment drawing nearer with each second. I thought of just rushing out of the house, perhaps shouting that I had forgotten something vitally important. Then I glanced out of the window and saw a young, tall woman coming up the garden path towards the house. She was dark, and wore a plain purple-coloured coat. She waved her hand, smiling at me through the window. A few seconds later my torment had ended and everything became amazingly natural and easy.

'You poor boy,' she laughed, coming into the room. 'How long have you been waiting for me? I window-shopped – I'm always doing that. Look what you're reading! Hasn't Mother given you anything better than that? Have you really been reading it, Louis, after all the things you called them – remember?' She was laughing all the time, her large eyes shining mischievously.

'Don't remind me,' I said, amazed at my boldness.

She went on to talk about some local art exhibition she had seen in Nottingham, just before coming away, and she pulled a wry face. 'Ugh! There was only one I liked, of a terribly thin greyhound with a colour like diarrhoea!' she cried, and laughed gaily, like a schoolgirl.

Afterwards I remember asking her if she had talked so

much and at such great speed in order to put me at my ease. Surely she must have noticed.

'No, I didn't notice,' she admitted. 'I was too nervous myself! That's why I couldn't stop talking, you see. It always affects me like that – the more nervous I am the faster I go.'

'I wouldn't have thought you were nervous,' I said. And she became suddenly serious, giving me a grim little smile.

'I live on my nerves,' she said simply.

Her mother came back into the room to ask if we were staying for dinner, or going out somewhere. I found myself wondering what Stella had told her, to explain things. I was amazed that everything was so natural, as if I were a friend of the family.

Stella turned to me. 'Where are we going, Louis?' she asked naïvely. I suggested taking a bus to the outskirts, and then a walk in the country, as the weather was fine. We only had a few hours.

'Lovely,' she said. 'We'll get a meal out somewhere,' she told her mother.

I didn't really see our surroundings. I was too aware of her. I stared at things without comprehending them. After she had gone back I went home with my mind dazed, feeling like a man, a lord, a man of the world, mellow with all the experience that life could offer. Probably I was more naïve and confused than ever, but none of that mattered in my exultant mood. The whole world was like a fruit, waiting. I had been treated with respect, even admiration, and my seriousness – always a stumbling-block – had been accepted and taken for granted. I had been befriended by a woman of the world, and it had made a man out of me.

I resumed our correspondence ardently, with plenty of fuel now to throw on the fire. I made references to her appearance, modelling and perfecting her face in my imagination. Supremely confident, I said whatever I liked, not caring what chances I took. In a very short time I had exalted everything about her into shining virtues, for I couldn't forget her warm, affectionate treatment of me. It was my first success, so it kept resounding in me, feeding my hopes.

One day I had a rather cold, arrogant letter from her, and it enraged me so much that I sat down immediately at the table to reply. I wanted to provoke her in some way, force her to show her feelings by some profound shock. The anger seething in me gave me a wonderful feeling of reckless indifference and irresponsibility, and I told her that was hopelessly in love with her. Later, as I repeated it to myself, wondering what I had done, it began to root itself firmly in me as a truth, staying behind after my indignation had died away.

'For God's sake,' she answered at once, 'don't ever write like that again – it's dynamite. There's something you don't know about – perhaps I shall tell you one day, when I feel I can really trust you. One thing I have vowed to do, and that is, never hurt him again in that way. I would rather die. So please understand, and don't write such things – will you promise?'

This sounded ominous and final – the end of my advances before they had even begun. But I read a suppressed excitement between the lines, and I was not mistaken. In her very next letter she was 'feeling mad, because it's September – that month always makes me a little crazy', and suggesting a secret meeting at Nottingham the following Saturday night. 'If you are as insane as I am, and think it's worth it, travelling sixty miles just to see me for a couple of hours – then come!' It was the intrigue and the challenge that she was unable to resist.

And this time I had come to live here, uninvited. I blinked, lying there in the darkness in a strange bed. I was certainly mad.

The next morning, when I went down for my breakfast, there was no sign of the old man.

'Mister's gone to the corner for his paper – always the same. He likes to do it – gives him something to do,' chuckled his wife, scurrying round me as I sat at the table. 'Are you all right? You like porridge, don't you? That's good, that's good. How about bacon and egg, a piece of toast? Here he comes now!' And she darted into the poky hole of a kitchen, making signs at me over her shoulder. I heard the fumbling sounds approaching down the passage again, and then he entered the room. He seemed even bigger than I had remembered him. In one hand he grasped a knotted stick, in the other his morning paper, and still he wore the cloth cap which I had never seen off his head. I wondered if he was bald. He stood a moment, towering over me in the middle of the room, breathing heavily. I tried not to look at his great belly, but my eyes were straying to it of their own accord, so I had to say quickly:

'Good morning. That's a nice stick you've got.'

'Morning, young man.' He swayed past me dangerously, making for his armchair. I began to regret my remark, wondering if I had been too familiar. He lowered himself painfully, letting out a huge sigh. Then he muttered in a low voice, as if to himself:

'D'you say you like my stick, then?'

He had caught me with my mouth full of food, but I felt that he was waiting urgently for my answer, that it was somehow important to him, so I managed to say, 'Yes, very much. It looks a good one. Have you had it a long time?' I looked across, and he was gazing down at his paper as if engrossed in it.

'Aye,' he said, in a voice that was barely audible. Then he bawled out: 'Missus! What about me bloody tea!'

I was anxious to go now. I gave the old woman some money in advance; she seemed to handle the whole business. Then she fetched a grubby visitors' book from upstairs for me to sign.

'We have to keep it, the police make us,' she said, apologetically.

Her husband had got up silently, and he came over and stood watching. The old woman nudged him and cuddled his arm as I wrote down my name and address.

I stepped into the street. The light was grey; everything seemed cold and clammy, shrunken. It was like being in a damp room. The sky itself was soiled and old, damp and gritty, the dirty buildings poking up into it thickly. I shivered and hurried along the pavement. I had known hundreds of days, just like this one, in Coventry and London. It was as if the very light had at last become impregnated with soot, choking and burying the sun forever. It was nearly ten in the morning, but it could have been any time. The little patches of garden in front of each house, with pathetic colourless plants struggling to stay alive, had an almost indecent look to them; they were so naked and exposed, such a succession of identical stories, a mournful repetition of the same wretched tune. Nobody bothered to keep off the dogs, or pick up the dirty scraps of paper blowing in, lodging between the railings.

I told myself I was a fool to hurry; I had plenty of time if I was to stick to my original plan of intercepting Stella outside the school. Wandering about, I came to the Public Reading Room, and walked in. I could see if there were any suitable jobs.

It was a long, pleasant building, a wing of the main library. The tables and newspaper stands were of a reddish wood, and there were large windows along one wall.

After making a few notes I began to get bored. No wonder, I told myself, when really you don't want a job at all. Also I knew perfectly well the weeks and months and years of boredom and frustration lying behind these innocent few lines of print. And my resolve to get a job immediately, to get back in harness again, began to weaken. I realized what I had escaped. I even made one or two mental calculations, to determine how long I could make my savings last, with careful economy. Then the whole thing wearied me and

I turned to the personal column for a breath of human interest.

Almost the first advertisement I caught sight of made me blink, and look again, more intently:

> – 'Four men, creative, spiritual group, looking for financial backing. Manuscripts and over fifty paintings may be inspected.'

I read it through again, then a third time, before I could absorb it. It seemed preposterous in cold print, among all the columns of commercial stuff. Gradually, as I stood staring at it, wondering if it really was a proof of another world existing quite apart from the industrious ruts of these pages, or if I had read far too much into it, the conviction grew slowly stronger in me that I should be caught up with these unknown men and their lives. I was meant to stumble on them. There was no address, simply a box number, which I jotted down. It was the combination of words in the advert that fascinated me, though I mistrusted it. If the word 'creative' had been there alone, I should have concluded at once that it was just another art group struggling to establish itself; if only the word 'spiritual' had been there, it would have conjured up in my mind a bunch of pseudo-religious cranks, something altogether repellent to me, a harking back to Blake and Yeats – that sort of thing. I was attracted to the curious linking of the two words. As it was, both words repulsed me a little, but I tried to be fair, to accept it as it stood. After all, it was difficult to phrase such an announcement in any other way, keeping it brief and to the point – assuming, of course, that they meant what I hoped they did. And what was that? It was hard to say. I knew what it was, but it was hard to bring out into the open. Perhaps something like Van Gogh's dream – his 'atelier of the South'. I thought, 'Who doesn't have such dreams, when they are isolated, and when everything is against it? It is clearly impossible, ridiculous, so we desire it more fervently, as a man sometimes creates his whole hope out of misfortunes.' Thinking back on it now, I am amazed that such a desire existed in me, so firmly rooted and passionate. I had always prided myself on a proud individuality. It was a habit of thought, an instinct, telling me to keep apart, and it gave me a proud, shut face. Then, out of nowhere, there was this desire.

I grew so excited that I ran out to a newsagent's shop around the corner and bought a writing-pad and a packet of envelopes. Then I went back and scribbled a quick note, saying that I was interested and should like further details. I made no reference to my financial state because I wanted to be sure of a reply. When I had posted it I felt relieved, and a little later I began to cool down considerably about the whole thing. Probably I was imagining all sorts of possibilities that could never come to anything, I told myself. I had walked into the small park behind the library and was sitting on an iron seat.

Sitting there, I became restless and preoccupied, thinking that I should soon be meeting Stella. I forgot all about the four men.

Chapter 5

I HAD already begun the journey across the city to the suburb where she lived, when the thought struck me that it was Easter-time. The schools would be closed, the children on holiday. I halted where I was, outside Woolworth's, stunned by the violent shock of this realization, my plan smashed to pieces at one blow. I had intended to walk all the way, so that I should get to know a few streets. People crowded past me on the pavement as I stood there, too dazed to think. I understood with one part of my mind that I should have to wait two or three weeks, and started to move on, refusing to believe it. Yet I felt a surge of relief because now I was spared an ordeal, because it was all postponed. Then after a few minutes I stopped again, cursing this development and disgusted with myself for being glad, for clutching at straws. I knew my loneliness would triumph very soon and make me want to meet her again more urgently than ever. Inexplicably wretched and baffled, I turned back. As I headed back in the direction of the square, I kept telling myself contemptuously that I should have gone on and waited outside the house until she came out. But the impracticability of such a scheme defeated me, as I secretly hoped it would. She might not come out all day; and people would grow suspicious of someone hanging about for hours at a street corner. I had to wait.

Not knowing what to do with myself, I had a meal at Lyons, then went into a cinema opposite, the Odeon. I sat in my plush seat in the hot darkness, wondering what I should do every night. I couldn't stay at my lodgings, even if the old people wanted me to. Nobody could sit there every night in that dim hole. The idea of taking a bed-sitting-room swam into my mind, and though I brushed aside the difficulty of the expense, it was such a bleak prospect that I couldn't face that either. I had had a furnished room in London.

The problem refused to be solved, so I gave it up. Sitting in the false warmth and oblivion of the cinema, it was easy to forget whatever waited outside.

When I returned to my lodgings that night, the old man, as he opened the door, gave me a surprise.

'You'll have a pal tonight,' he said, and gave me a fantastic wink.

'Oh yes?' I said, not knowing what to expect, following him slowly as he groped along towards the chink of light under the living-room door. His great bulk filled the passage, which was unlighted, so that I seemed to be following a moving piece of darkness.

He had opened the door. 'Here he is,' I heard him grunt without turning his head. He was speaking to his wife or the new lodger.

As I entered the dim room, which struck me as more shamefully bare each time I saw it, a young, fair-haired man sprang to his feet with obvious relief. He had been sitting on the dilapidated sofa.

'Hallo, there,' he cried, wrinkling his babyish forehead. He cried out his greeting as though he were overjoyed to see me, as if he'd been waiting months for this pleasure.

'I'm Harold Day!' he said, his voice rising, and he thrust

out his hand. Bewildered, I grasped it slackly, feeling slightly foolish, like a captain at a cricket match.

'I'm Louis Paul,' I said, cursing him for making me say my name out loud.

'Yes, I know; I've seen it in the book,' he cried, in a gushing, cultivated voice, smiling broadly and letting his eyes slide from my face to the old man's, back to mine and then away again, around the room somewhere. He was making me dizzy.

'I've just arrived,' he went on. 'Came up on the London train – and you got here yesterday, didn't you?'

He said all this in a disarming way, and with such eagerness that I almost believed for a moment that he knew me. His whole face shone with friendship. He was certainly intent on making a friend of me if possible – probably because the old man's company had unnerved him. He started to tell me about himself with amazing openness, quite oblivious of his surroundings, and ignoring the old man completely, who had settled himself in his corner, by the gigantic, intense heap of red fire, to watch us, pretending to fill his pipe.

'Yes, I've just come up from London today – I'm from the Slade. Been there three years, more or less. I'm a sculptor. At least, I want to be – I hope to be, rather. Yes, I'm the advanced guard really, my wife will follow with the child, when I've found a flat for us. Do you know this town at all?'

'Hardly at all,' I said, falling into his way of speaking.

'I've got a job at Boots' factory, you see – teaching Art at their new workers' educational school at Beeston – sort of experimental. Should be very interesting. What I really want do, though, when we get settled in, is find a place where I can do my sculpture. That's my real work.'

He chatted on to me so unselfconsciously that I looked at him in astonishment. It sounded so fantastic to me, his talk, in that mean room. I did not want to be linked with him, yet he almost had his arm round my shoulder. I didn't care what he said when we were alone, but in front of the two old people it made me squirm and feel ashamed. It was laughable, yet it was idiotic too, the way this fellow was behaving. Couldn't he see how meagre it was here? Couldn't he grasp that he was at the bottom of existence in this poor room? Was he blind? He talked as if life was a game.

I made some excuse and went up to the bedroom, though it was still fairly early. Harold trotted after me like a dog, anxiously keeping me in sight. I began to feel better about him. Now I had got him out of that room, I was glad of his company.

Sitting on the bed, I said, 'How did you land up here?' I grinned at him.

He was foraging in a very new-looking rucksack which he had on the floor between his legs. He looked up, startled.

'Here? Well I went to the Y.M.C.A., and they . . .'

'Same here,' I laughed. 'What d'you think of it, this place?'

'What do I think of it?' Harold hesitated. He didn't care to commit himself.

'Yes,' I said. 'Not exactly home from home, is it?'

'Well, no,' he admitted, frowning and looking uncomfortable, as though I had touched on something problematic. 'Still, I musn't complain; it's only for a few days, till I find a flat somewhere.' He looked across at me hopefully. 'I suppose you don't know of anywhere?'

'Afraid not,' I said. 'I'm a stranger, practically.' Then something made me plunge on. 'I was interested in what you said downstairs, though, about your being a sculptor.'

He beamed at me. 'Oh, really? Do you do anything yourself?'

'Not much. I've tried my had at a few water-colours, that's about all. I haven't been to an art school, though,' I added awkwardly. I had meant to be apologetic, but it sounded arrogant, so I blundered on, 'I don't know that I want to, but sometimes I think I'd like to go to one or two life classes, and perhaps do a bit of modelling.'

I wondered why I was telling him all this. Yet I hadn't told him my real reason for not going to an art school. Apart from lack of time, I had always fought shy of a class of students, imagining them all to be first-class draughtsmen, budding Leonardos. I was afraid of looking like a clumsy fool.

'How interesting!' said Harold. A light sprang into his eyes. Now it did not seem so far from the Slade after all. 'Perhaps I can see some of your work one day? I should like to very much, if I may.'

'It isn't what you'd call work,' I laughed, 'but you can have a look at it, certainly, when I'm settled. I've got to send for things like that; they're at home at the moment. I'm like you at the present time. No fixed abode.'

'I see; yes of course. You know, I think the life-class idea is an excellent one. Excellent! I must make arrangements to go to some evening classes myself, I need the practice badly – getting rusty.'

'I dare say.'

Harold lifted his head.

'We must go along together!' he suggested brightly.

'Yes,' I said, non-commital. Then on an impulse I added, 'What about tomorrow night? We could go and inquire; no harm in that, anyway.' I suddenly saw it as a partial solution of my problem. It would be somewhere to go for one evening.

'Why, yes,' Harold said. He seemed less enthusiastic now it had become so definite.

Suddenly I felt exhausted. I got into bed. Harold was still digging things out of his rucksack. I could hear a steady metallic ticking, and I knew there was no clock in the room.

'Is that a clock you've got there?'

'Yes, old man – an alarm clock. I've got two.'

'Two?'

'Well, I'm rather a heavy sleeper, and one clock isn't very reliable, so I set them both. I put them half an hour ahead of the other.'

'I see.'

'I hope it won't disturb you,' he added anxiously, and I had to laugh. It was his high voice, and the thought of that clacking shaft and pulley outside the window.

'No, that's all right,' I said.

By raising my head very slightly I could see him, over by the door, pulling off his trousers. He stepped out of them so gingerly that I almost burst out laughing again. Before I lay back I saw a pair of spotlessly clean pyjamas laid out in neat lines, and a dark red dressing-gown hung over the bed-rail.

Harold switched off the light, and everything at once became more cheerful. The room lost its grey, mildewed, sepulchral appearance. I lay in the clean dark, listening to him winding his two clocks. Two clocks! I must remember that, I chuckled to myself. I lay awake thinking about him, about our arrangement to go to the art school, gradually warming to him because he was harmless and friendly. A tremor of excitement ran through me, and the vague premonition of some kind of adventure unfolding, of things about to happen to me. I felt on the brink of something.

But art classes! It was unreal to me. I tried to imagine how I should act there, and it made me go cold. I remember that Stella had often urged me to go; she would have been delighted. At the beginning I had sent her a few of my water-colours – that was before we had met. They had surprised her, she wrote; she hadn't expected anything so bold and strong. She may have used the word crude, but not in a contemptuous way. And she detected a certain quality in them which made her wonder if I was a West Indian, or a negro, she told me afterwards.

'You mean to say you still kept on writing, thinking it may be a negro who was interested in you?' I asked her.

'Why not?' she said. 'Coloured men have always attracted me.'

I could never make her understand my aversion to art-school training, the whole principle of it. It was something quite apart from my fear of being made to look a fool. When I tried to explain that I could only work from my feelings – that I was a 'belly painter' as she put it – she made an angry movement of her hands. 'I know all about that,' she said in a steely voice, 'I've heard it all before and I agree with you, but without proper training, without knowledge, you're as handicapped as if you had no hands or feet. You're just hit-or-miss.'

She always used language with precision, almost callously, as if she were in a court of law. She hammered her points home. It was a sign of her strong will, which was like a man's; and that was why her letters, when they arrived, nearly always chilled me. They left me devoid of emotion, until there came a reaction of anger.

It was different when I heard her voice. Hearing its warmth and femininity, I was able to offset the efficiency of her language. But her letters, without this voice, were maddening things. Time after time I was made fiendish with hate because of their inhuman look. I felt it was monstrous and freakish for a woman to write letters like that. I often told her so, but I don't think she ever really understood what I was raging about. And it became a vicious circle; the more wild and accusing my replies were, the more clipped and shorn of all feelings her letters became. Yet when I wanted to put a stop to it, as something senseless and perverse, I found I had developed a sort of furtive appetite for it. I was deliberately drawing these barbed words to myself, even though I longed to get away and finish everything.

'Coloured men have always attracted me.' How

characteristic of her that was. She was perfectly serious. 'I like their faces; so sensual,' she said.

'I must have been a disappointment, then,' I said, teasing her.

She smiled faintly. 'Oh no. There's something of that about your looks too – didn't you know? And you're pale, and dark, and you're slim. All those qualities have a strong attraction for me.'

I was flattered by these remarks, yet they exasperated me. And I took everything she said seriously, though she was often momentary. I had never known anyone like her before. To be liked for the particular 'qualities' I had, my pallor, dark hair, thinness, and so on, was something I could not stand. I wanted to be liked as a human being. I don't believe she expected this revolt, but it hardly ruffled her. Sometimes I could have bitten off my tongue. I kept poisoning and killing what genuine feeling there was between us, and with one half of my nature I wanted it to go on. Her sophisticated flattery was a balm to me, and sometimes I fairly rejoiced in my power, for I could see that I did genuinely attract her. But the plebeian in me, the mongrel, kept revolting and overturning everything.

Deep within I knew it was all a poor substitute for what I really wanted, and this knowledge, like a rod, kept prodding at my conscience, bringing out the lout in me. I felt somehow cheapened and degraded.

One evening, after a bad argument, I found myself saying, as brutally as I could: 'I feel dirty with you. You make me feel dirty inside. Haven't you had enough intrigue now, with me?

51

What more do you want? What kind of man do you take me for?'

Her face changed visibly, becoming steely and hard in an instant. I stood watching her in horror, realizing that I had hurt her deeply at last, probably for the first time, and that she would never forget it. I wanted to soften what I had said, but her terrible expression made it impossible for me to speak. I looked dumbly as she waited a few seconds; then she turned on her heel and walked quickly away.

Afterwards things went on as before, on the surface. But I knew she hadn't forgiven me.

'No, Louis,' she said coldly, when I made an attempt to explain: 'I've had enough words from you. You've said everything now, haven't you? Don't worry about it; I've already forgotten what you said.' Then she said, with heavy sarcasm, 'You wouldn't come if you didn't want to see me, would you?'

I stared blankly at her. Was it as simple as that? Then I understand that all the time I was trying to change her, to make her into something else. I should never be able to accept her as she was.

I went away then, to London. The letters began again, to and fro. It made me think of a devilish pendulum that had got out of control.

I moved restlessly on the bed. There was no sound from Harold now. He lay perfectly still and silent.

I had spun a web for myself, I thought; and this conclusion shocked me with its startling clarity. Why meet her at all? Why go back there? And I almost groaned aloud. I would go back simply because there was no one else.

'You poor boy,' I whispered in the darkness, jeering at myself. Then I fell asleep.

The next evening I went along with Harold to the College of Art to make a few enquiries and enrol if possible. Harold carried a sketch-block. He had heard during the day that a life-class would be in progress this evening, and wanted to start immediately, if he could.

'I don't want to go regularly, or anything like that,' he explained to me. 'That's such a bore, really. If I can wander in every so often, and make a few studies, it'll keep me in practice. A sculptor must draw and draw, you know. He can't do enough life-drawing. And they usually let you come and go when you feel like it at these places. They've always let me wander in, wherever I've been. They understand.'

He was still talking volubly as we passed through the big wrought-iron gates, our feet crunching the gravel, and began to mount the broad white steps. I was in no mood for conversation. Even in Harold's company I felt tense and nervous, gutted inside. When I saw the pompous building, such an edifice of petrified Art, I had to screw up my courage. Yet I wanted the experience, and this time I was determined to go through with it. I told myself I should never have such favourable circumstances again, and marched into the vestibule as grim as a martyr.

Harold went forward confidently. He was talking excitedly to the girl behind the inquiry desk when a stiff, middle-aged man walked up and interrupted him. I hadn't noticed him approaching and I stood back a little, not liking the look of him. His head was round and compact-looking. He looked very efficient.

'Is there anything I can do?' he rapped, and introduced himself. He was the head of some department, which explained his air of authority. He had short, bristly hair, turning grey, and a reddish moustache, clipped short. There was a strong Northern burr in his speech.

'As I was explaining to the young lady,' Harold resumed smoothly, 'all we want, actually my friend and I, is to have access to the life class now and then, and . . .'

'You can't do that,' the man barked. His eyes glinted shrewdly with a mixture of amusement and irritation.

Harold paused, frowning slightly. Then he plunged on again as though nothing had happened.

'Er – you see, this is the point. I've just come up from the Slade – I'm a sculptor – and I teach at Boots' – experimental work, you know. What I should like to do is make few studies –'

'You can make as many studies as you like,' the man interrupted again, this time with deliberate rudeness, 'but you can't just drift in and out. You'll have to enrol for the whole session or not at all. That clear?'

He gave Harold a quick, contemptuous look. In a way I felt sympathy for the man, though he was making me angry. Probably he hated Londoners, and ex-Slade students especially. No doubt he detests artists more than anything else, I thought, and tried to imagine what it would be like, having to deal with artists in bud all your life.

'Thank you,' said Harold, becoming very reserved and haughty. 'I understand.'

The man grinned at both of us. 'Righto!' he cried cheerily. He marched on down the corridor.

'What do you want to do, then?' I said to Harold, who was looking at me appealingly. 'Shall we enrol?'

He blinked, then shifted about uncomfortably in his clothes, as though he wanted to avoid making a decision.

'I didn't really want to take the full course, you see,' he wavered.

'It doesn't matter, as far as I'm concerned,' I argued, beginning to get irritable. 'I shan't turn up if I don't want to, so what difference does it make?'

But he was still hesitant, so I said emphatically, 'Let's enrol,' and went up to the desk to pay over my money. I guessed that this would make him decide, and I was right.

We began to wander down a maze of corridors. I led the way, feeling resolute now, after our little encounter with authority. I would go through with it now on principle.

I stopped a moment while Harold halved his sketch-block to provide me with materials. When we eventually found the life-room the class had already started. The only space available was against the wall towards the rear, just in from the door. All the students were bowed over their work, drawing intently from the model, and no one bothered to look up as we edged our way in. I was relieved, and began to enjoy myself, looking round at everything, fascinated. My first impressions cheered me up tremendously; I was gladdened by the informality of things, the drawings pinned up on the pale walls, the students balancing drawing-boards on their knees, or using chair-backs for supports, and using any medium they fancied. There was no sign of a teacher. I approved of it all.

When I became fairly settled and more at ease I started to look at the model. I grinned to myself, thinking of the reactions of my ex-workmates at the factory if I were to tell them about this; though it was quite true, as Stella had said: a model sits so still she is like something carved out of stone. I found it hard to believe she was alive. And the classical pose completed the illusion. Once she moved very slightly and I stared harder, wondering if my eyes were playing tricks on me.

Leaning forward in my chair, I peered over the shoulder of the girl in front of me, curious to see her drawing. For the past ten minutes I hadn't seen her lift her head once. She was working meticulously in pen and Indian ink, like a medical artist. The head in her drawing was finished off completely ,to the last detail, but I could see no sign of the body. A few minutes later, when I glanced over again, she had added on the neck and one shoulder. She was putting the figure together piece by piece, like an engineer, adding on each component perfectly finished. I was so astonished and so pleased to find a regular art student doing such a mad thing that I turned to Harold, intending to whisper the news to him. When I saw his own lifeless piece of work I changed my mind. Good God, I thought, are these the Michaelangelos I was so concerned about, who were going to make me look ridiculous? I looked again at my own drawing. It was no better than theirs, but it was no worse. And I felt I could do better if the pose was less boring.

The teacher came in and called for a break. He wore a neat grey suit and looked like a clerk. Moving stiffly, the model struggled to her feet, and a girl walked languidly over to her with a thick brown dressing-gown. It was all done smoothly, with tact and delicacy, in a few seconds, the model sitting clothed in a corner, English and respectable, chatting in a low voice to some young students. Even though I had seen her move about naked, I still couldn't cast off the statue illusion. It was uncanny. She was a dark, sullen girl of about seventeen, quite plump, with surprisingly heavy breasts and lovely fresh skin. Her hair was untidy, and she kept running her fingers through it as a man would. I stared at her loutishly because it was all strange and fascinating to me. I noticed that she still maintained her blank, sullen expression, as if afraid to relax, knowing she would be back on the 'throne' again in a few minutes.

The teacher was wandering round the room casually, looking at the work and offering friendly suggestions. He was an affable, rather timid man, youngish, and wore glasses. He talked softly in a jerky, nervous manner, very self-conscious and apprehensive. I watched him without concern as he came slowly nearer; I had no fears now about my own drawing, after seeing specimens of the others. And the informal atmosphere, the lack of real seriousness, encouraged me to relax and gaze around, absorbing impressions. Harold was talking earnestly to his right-hand neighbour about the various theories of drawing.

Coming up to Harold and myself, the friendly teacher introduced himself and then wrote our names in his register. When he looked at my drawing, standing behind me and leaning down with his pencil, he said, 'Yes, yes, oh yes, I think you've perhaps got it; yes, I think so, I think so – don't you? There's just something *here* – er – something I *think* you might have missed – er – possibly. Just . . . just a feeling – yes, definitely, I think, definitely a feeling *there* – like this, perhaps!' And leaning down stiffly, he made several bold sweeping curves around the thighs and knees of my figure. I suppose it was to give it solidity.

'Don't you agree there's a feeling there?' he intoned mildly, his face fixed securely in its friendliness, turned slightly away. Before I could answer he had wandered off.

I watched him arranging the model in her new pose. As he did so, one of the male students to my left was whispering loudly to a companion, 'Look at him, he's a scream all right! Look, he's afraid to touch her – he's scared stiff!'

It was true. He was getting nowhere, moving around in front of her, making vague suggestions and doing his best not to meet the girl's rigid stare. He murmured, 'Not quite like that, I don't think – do you? Perhaps a little to the left with that arm – er – no . . . a little to the right, I should say . . .'

Somebody giggled. 'Go on, grab it!' hissed the student to my left. 'Go on, Leslie; it won't bite!'

At last he had managed it. He was red and flustered, and almost bolted from the room. I felt sorry for him. What a fool he was! He only showed his face once more, very briefly, to tell us it was time to leave.

On the way back to our lodgings, Harold surprised me by announcing that he had found a small flat, 'in a nice part of the town, quite inexpensive'. Someone at work had told him about it, and he had gone straight there during his lunch hour to see if it was any good.

'I'm sure we can make it comfortable, when my wife arrives. You must come and visit us, my friend, when we're settled in. Come along any time.'

He was certainly in a hurry. He had already sent for his family, and the following day he moved in. I always meant to go and see him – it would have been somewhere to go – but I never did.

We had reached Shakespeare Street and were strolling towards the Y.M.C.A., taking our time. It was a beautiful night, clear and silent, blooming over us like an enormous blue-black flower. I looked up into its depths, and blundered into my companion.

'Sorry,' I said. 'I'm not drunk. I can't take my eyes off those stars. Look at them!'

'Yes, aren't they beautiful – beautiful.' And he went on talking excitedly about the evening's adventures, telling me how good it was to be back in the art-school atmosphere again.

'You really miss it, you know – though it's hard to explain just what it is. I suppose that sounds silly to you,' he added, and blushed suddenly. He gave me a shy look.

'No, I think I know what you mean,' I said hastily, not knowing what to do with him when he blushed.

59

As we came up to the house at Shakespeare Villas his conversation sounded suddenly ridiculous, and I felt the urge to prod him sharply back to harsh reality by some remark. Pointing at the house I said, 'God, look at it! It looks more naked than that model.' Harold lifted his hand to his mouth and made a sort of snuffling laugh. Which made me wish I had said something really excessive. In the starlight, under all that beauty, the house did look utterly naked, somehow stripped and shameful, and almost disgustingly ugly. It seemed to beg for the shroud of darkness to cover it.

Chapter 6

THE old man – I never knew his name – had another piece of news for me when he let us into the house. 'Somebody's been here looking for you. Queer bloke. Got a beard – funny looking chap he was,' he mumbled, as we trailed after him towards the living-room. I had entered first, and was directly behind him in the dark passage, so I concluded that he was talking to me.

'Does he mean me or you, do you think?' chirped Harold over my shoulder, as though the man was stone deaf. Disgusted with him, I thought of giving a backward lunge with my foot to shut him up. 'I don't know anybody with a beard, do I?' I heard him murmuring, behind me.

But in the room the old man handed me a card. On it was printed: 'Jack Kelvin – scenic artist.' An address had been scribbled in ink underneath the name, and underlined heavily. Harold stood watching curiously as I tried to absorb it – I believe he still thought there was some absurd mistake, that the card should have gone to him.

The old man's wife had come to my side. She tugged at my coat sleeve excitedly.

'Go away, Missus,' the husband said, settling massively in his corner.

But out of a bright face she cried, 'He's a strange young man, a funny fellow with a beard. He says he wants you to go and see him; he says you wrote him a letter – that's right, isn't it, Mister? Yes, of course it is! He's an interesting young man; he talked to me about religion, about all kinds of things

61

– You was out!' she almost screeched, flinging these last words at the old man, who sat with a shut face by the fire, ignoring her. 'You wasn't here; you don't know!' she cried in triumph. And turning to me, peering up into my face, she said indulgently, 'I told him. He was out,' as if excusing an imbecile.

I had realized by now that it concerned the four men of the advert that I had answered. I had forgotten it completely. There was a tense silence, and I knew that I should have to say something. Not knowing how to extricate myself, and unable to offer any explanation which would make sense, I merely stammered. 'Yes – thank you – I remember now. I'd forgotten all about him – I'll go tomorrow night.'

I threw out this morsel of information as a sort of compromise, smiling round at everybody ceremoniously. Harold had sat down on the sofa, looking slightly crestfallen. The old woman stood looking at me with her head cocked on one side, waiting for me to go on. There was a general air of expectancy in the room which began to unnerve me.

'Well,' I said loudly, 'I'm dog-tired. I'll turn in, I think.'

And I said my good nights quickly and went up to bed, leaving Harold to his fate.

I never saw him again. When he came upstairs I must have been asleep. And in the mornings he always got up earlier than me, to go off to work. Even his alarm clock failed to wake me this last time, and when I returned from Jack Kelvin's the following evening he had already packed his rucksack and moved to his new address.

I could have gone to Kelvin's house at any time during that day, which was a Friday, but I thought it best to wait until the evening. My feet refused to take me there until then, in any case, because of nervousness, but this time I had a strong desire to go there, and now that Harold Day had departed, I needed friends badly. And I was curious to meet this man, after the descriptions I had heard. Some of the old excitement began to run through me again, which I had felt when I first saw the advert. By the evening my usual fear of meeting strangers had dwindled away. I had been doing nothing all day, only wandering through the streets and into the Castle grounds for an hour or two, until it started to rain. This drove me into a second-hand bookshop near a huge, placarded dance-hall. I stayed in there a long time, losing all sense of time. Then I began to feel hungry, and found a small restaurant in a narrow, cobbled lane choked with high buildings. This was in a historical part of the city called the Lace Market.

At about seven I sat in a bus travelling towards Jack Kelvin's address. In a matter of minutes I found myself in one of the poorer districts. There was a sense of vacancy and squalor, a terrible hurting ugliness always before the eyes, the bus running over the disused tramlines, past meat shop and chemists' shops, and shops jammed with worthless junk, second-hand clothes and worm-eaten furniture.

'Get off at the Grand – I'll tell you when,' said the conductor, when I told him the name of the street.

As we turned sharply and gathered speed, rattling down a long, grey hill lined with poor shops, he yelled out:

'Grand!'

And I got to my feet. We came to a halt just beyond a set of traffic lights, and I jumped off, finding myself almost at the entrance of the 'Grand', a tiny ramshackle cinema with an arc of coloured electric bulbs, next to the local Co-operative.

For a few moments, as I hesitated on the pavement under a street lamp, there was a lull in the traffic at this crossroads, and the nearest pedestrian was two hundred yards away. The traffic lights snapped on and off senselessly. I had a weird sense of being observed. Then I noticed the cashier at the top of the cinema steps, gazing out forlornly through her grill. Yet I still thought I could feel something else.

I called out to the woman, asking for directions, and the sound of my own voice appalled me, it was so pitiful, human, weak. Was it as obvious to the woman as it was to me? Feeling certain it was, I almost ran from that place, confused and ashamed. The very electricity shedding light down on me seemed to be stripping me naked where I stood.

Moving up the main street, seeking a turning to the left, I wondered if I had heard the woman's directions correctly. Had she said left or right? But I had no intention of going back.

The street I wanted was called Hyson Terrace. I had reached it by a roundabout way, for the bottom end of it ran into the big bisecting road, only a few yards from the traffic lights. It was a fairly long side-street, with two identical rows of tall, grimy houses, the door flush with the pavement. At

64

the top end it narrowed suddenly and lost itself in a maze of lanes and alleys, the buildings all different and irregular, their roofs at different levels. Probably this was why there was no sign of any traffic, because the street led nowhere. It was a dreary backwater, with life trapped and stagnating in it, behind the aspidistras and soiled curtains. It depressed me, yet there was a lurking sort of enjoyment in me, too, because I was reminded of the streets of my childhood.

I became gradually more and more tense and nervous as I approached Jack Kelvin's house, examining the card in my hand every few yards.

Struggling to keep a calm face, I banged firmly on the door. My other hand was trembling. I tried bunching it into a fist, and when that failed I let it hang loose, the fingers dangling. But nothing I did was of any use. I found myself glaring at it almost in hatred, as though it had a life apart from me. Then the door moved. My heart lurched in my chest.

The man in the doorway gave me a wry, twisted smile, and said immediately:

'You're Louis Paul. Step inside. *Entrez!*' And I believe I felt a smile curving my own lips impulsively, despite my nervousness. I had never seen such a cunning, wary look on a man's face before, and the laughable thing was that it seemed so transparent, so theatrical. I thought he was trying to make me laugh, but he was perfectly serious.

On a first impression it was his eyes, small and squinting, that struck me as being the main cause of that shifty expression. Yet afterwards he had that look about his whole person, with his queer, jerky movements of the body, and the furtive white face, adorned with long hair and a beard, and looking like something that peered startled out of a hole.

He was wearing a sort of sleeveless dressing-gown which just hung from his shoulders, unfastened, over his shirt and trousers. It seemed to be a home-made affair of bluish felt, tied around the middle with a length of pyjama cord. I wondered at this rather womanish addition, because its purpose was obviously to give the garment shape, not to fasten it.

He stepped nimbly to one side in the doorway and I walked in, making my way down the hallway to an open door I could see at the end. Kelvin banged the front door shut and charged after me.

'That's the one, that's it!' he shouted as I hesitated. '*Entrez!*'

There was someone else in the room, a young, lanky fellow, grinning in a friendly fashion, who sprang up from his seat as soon as I went through the door.

'Hallo,' he said warmly, and put out his hand. I grasped it with a blind, automatic movement, staring sightless into his face.

'My name's Keith Becker,' he said, drawling his words, and he pointed to a chair. 'Take a pew.'

He had a sunburnt face. I sat down blankly, blinking under the bright flood of light.

The room was as bare as the living-room at my lodgings. There were only the necessities, and the view from the window was very similar: another tiny, hemmed-in yard, leading out to the lavatory and dustbin, and chocolate-painted gate opening on a dirty entry. But in detail, in atmosphere, this room was quite different. A crude mask hung on one wall, grimacing, made of papier-mache and daubed with red, yellow and green paint. Then I saw the fire-screen in front of the fireplace, with the abstract design painted on it, purple and yellow. And along one wall, above a divan bed heaped with blankets and sheets, ran a shelf of books.

Jack Kelvin had sat down on this bed, facing me. He was running his fingers through his black hair, scowling down at his shoes. I looked at him quickly, noticing the nose, short and lumpy on the colourless, pock-marked face, and how red and wet his lower lip was, hanging slack in the scrubby beard.

Becker just grinned like an oaf, watching me carelessly. I guessed that he was waiting for me to speak. There was a strange, wary atmosphere. The queer silence lasted about a minute. I felt that the two men were waiting for me to declare myself, to betray my real character. It was more than mere curiosity. They were waiting to see if I came up to certain standards, certain requirements, of which I knew nothing – something in the nature of a test, which they regarded as essential. I was sure of it. And they were not going to speak, to give themselves away, until I had passed their test; I sensed that.

As well as this queer half-knowledge, I felt my position to be a false one, because of the business of the financial backing; I had made no reference to it in my reply to the advert. I was a sort of trespasser, I thought, so I blurted out:

'One thing I ought to tell you, about the money part of your advert. ... I'm afraid I haven't got any. I should have told you that before. All the same, I wanted to meet you, I was interested. It seemed to be in the cards? Does it make any difference?'

I was talking to Kelvin, who still stared down at the floor – sensing that he was the leader. Becker was smiling across at him. Still the man sat there inert. I saw it was a sort of game he was playing.

Suddenly he sat bolt upright on the bed, leaning forward and looking at me intensely.

'What cards?' he said, and glanced across slyly at Becker.

I stared at him blankly.

'Know anything about Tarot cards?' he asked.

I shook my head, smiling, beginning to understand.

'Doesn't matter. We knew you hadn't any money. I guessed as much when I went to your digs. The thing is, if we put an advert in the paper, and you answer it, then that's it. That's it for us. Eh, Keith?'

He winked at his friend, who laughed softly again. And as his manner grew more natural, less guarded – though he was never open with me – his speech took on a coarse, plebeian quality, earthy and utterly without culture, something I found strongly attractive. I took him now for a man of working-class origin, despite his appearance.

There was nothing honest about him. But his very craftiness had a touch of the comic about it, as though he had made up his mind to be like that, deliberately. Later, as I knew him more, I found him to be a person activated by all sorts of silly, idiotic theories – he kept thinking up new ones and discarding old ones, like a sort of chameleon philosopher. That was what he was up to now. Not understanding this, his behaviour only baffled me. I only realised that he was the leader, and wondered at him, responding to his strange half-genuine fervour. I was amused and full of questions, yet he troubled me. I allowed myself to go under his spell, as a man would give himself up to a circus performer. I sat very quiet within myself and looked and listened.

Keith Becker spoke in the same loud, heavy way as his friend, mouthing his words. But he was a sharp contrast as a man, not animated at all, slow and lazy in his movements. He sat now under the window, sprawled at ease in his chair, his long, heavy mouth hanging open rather stupidly, obviously taking pleasure in the little drama. He seemed to have no self-consciousness at all. But Kelvin was full of it; I expected his face to start twitching at any moment. His little eyes blinked incessantly as he stared at me, leaning forward with both hands on his knees.

In an attempt to ward off scrutiny and relieve the atmosphere, yet knowing I was being irrelevant, and that they were both waiting for something else from me, I said casually:

'I had a funny feeling as I came here, when I got off the bus in front of the Grand. As if somebody was watching me. There wasn't a soul about, though, just at that time.'

Kelvin roared with laughter.

'There was – it was me! I was in a shop doorway opposite. I wanted to get a good look at you before you arrived. Isn't that interesting! You knew then?' He scowled down at the floor, then glanced across with his face solemn. Then in a second his expression changed, and he was smiling wryly at me. 'I followed you all the way from there. When you took the wrong turn, I thought, "Christ, where's he off to now?" yet I knew it was you; it was written all over you. You were nervous as a cat. . . . Isn't that queer!'

This last phrase he addressed to Becker in a soft, hissing voice, lowering his voice confidentially, ignoring me. Becker just leaned back with his hands clasped and nodded, suddenly old and wise.

I looked from one to the other. The tenseness in the room had eased now, and I began to relax and feel pleasant and happy, triumphant. Though I was still outside their circle, not yet accepted, I felt somehow confident that I should be. The certainty glowed in me like a wine. I thought again that they were waiting for some sign from me, without even realizing it themselves.

There was another pause, an awkward, stupid silence. Kelvin's remark about my acute nervousness in the street had given me a nasty shock. 'So he notices such things,' I thought. And I watched him closely, with a new respect.

'What made you answer it?' Becker asked suddenly, drawling his question out. 'What did you think you'd find?'

Once again I was surprised. I had not expected such a penetrating, direct question to come from Becker. He didn't seem capable of it. He sat upright now, his long legs vertical.

I decided not to answer directly. Instead I said:

'I read a letter the other day that Van Gogh wrote – to Emile Bernard, I think – saying what a thing it would be, if only a number of painters could unite to do great things; to collaborate.'

There was a silence, full of listening and thinking. I looked out of the window, suddenly ruffled and unsure.

'He wasn't talking about painting – not about Art, anyway,' I added in a desperate last fling, in an effort to make my point. I started to stammer something else, but Kelvin's delighted bellow of laughter drowned it. I stared at him in confusion. He was still laughing with his mouth wide open, showing his big teeth, putting an intense muscular energy into the act. His great vulgar guffaw filled the room. I even found myself laughing in sympathy, not knowing why. Becker say back and enjoyed the spectacle, grinning broadly.

'I knew that was it, when you answered the advert,' Kelvin said. He was perfectly calm now. He spoke to me directly for the first time. 'I knew you were the one. Go on. Tell us something else. Tell us what writers you like, go on. Let's hear some more; we're getting interested.'

The mockery still clung to him, but now a vibrant note had entered his voice. He had ceased to be a clown, or an inquisitive animal. He looked at me with intense eyes, and a candour on his face. Yet something made me draw back a little.

'That won't take long,' I said. 'There aren't many. I daresay you'll think them an odd assortment. Men like Dostoevsky, Whitman, Nietzsche, Lawrence . . .'

I had brought on another fit of laughter with my words.

This time I was glad to hear it, and not confused. I took it as a sign of victory.

'This is too good to be true,' Kelvin spluttered and chuckled, turning to his friend. 'Don't you think so, Beck? Would you bloody well believe it!' he bawled out, and leapt to his feet. His face had gone bright, as though he had seen a vision. He started to prance about, waving his arms and talking furiously.

'It only goes to show you!' he shouted, stamping up and down. He was making the doors and windows rattle. 'Haven't I said all along, let things happen, don't force things? How many more times have we got to have this proved to us before it sinks in? What a silly pair of sods! *We* decide, we make up our own minds that we want money, and what happens? *He* turns up! Can we get it any plainer than that, Beck – don't you see what I'm driving at?' He leaned down over his friend, his face distorted in a snarl, the little eyes twitching madly. I wondered if he was infuriated with Becker or himself. I was staring in fascination at them both.

'If we only knew the signs, if we were adepts, we'd know!' he yelled towards the window, ignoring both of us. 'Let things decide, that's the ticket! Christ Almighty, Beck, we ought to know that by now – all we've got to do is wait. Just wait. Sit on our backsides.'

He went back and sat on the divan as though nothing had happened. Then he said abruptly, in a quiet voice:

'How about a cup of tea?'

He jumped up and went into the kitchen. I could hear

him moving about and rattling crockery together.

Becker had sat stolidly throughout the other's tirade, as though he had seen it all before. He still wore the same lazy grin. It occurred to me that Kelvin had perhaps lost his temper because of his friend's animal remoteness, his slow, bovine response.

He came back into the room with a surprisingly light step, carrying a loaded tray. There was a hint of the fastidious in his step. He had even sliced and buttered some brown bread. Pouring out the golden jet of tea, he muttered in my direction. 'You'll have to drink it without sugar. I've run out. Help yourself to the grub. Jam over in the cupboard there, if you want that.'

He handed me a cup and saucer. The handle was missing from the cup.

'Hard luck,' he said, noticing it, and gave a short laugh. 'Beck, grab your tea.'

He stood near the table with hunched shoulders, in the middle of the room, holding his cup and saucer. Obviously he was still preoccupied and excited by something. I think we were both expecting him to continue in some way. He was scowling through the window, his brow furrowed, raising the cup to his mouth absently.

We were all silent. There was a clock ticking somewhere out of sight.

'Come on, Jack,' said Becker, breaking the silence. He smiled across at me. 'Say it, Jack, for God's sake. We've got our tongues hanging out here, waiting for more. You've wetted out appetites for the Book of Revelation by St. Jack.'

Kelvin swung round. Then he turned aside, half-sheepishly.

'Oh, is that it?' he said, and laughed. He sounded tired. He returned to the bed and sat down. 'Not tonight, lads,' he said in a more cheerful voice. Then he lifted his head and looked at me questioningly. To my astonishment, I found myself speaking, as though he had compelled me.

'When I came tonight, I thought I might perhaps meet all four of you,' I said.

'No. We're split up. The other two don't get here very often. You'll meet them, though, if it's in the cards. One's a carpenter – he's not really an artist; more of a craftsman. But he's one of us all right; he sympathizes. That's right, isn't it, Beck? . . . The other one, he's the real painter. George – George Meluish. He's a queer bird all right; takes some fathoming. If he's in the mood he'll tell you some yarns – make your hair stand on end. Generally, though, he doesn't say very much. . . . The carpenter bloke, Cyril, he's got a workshop of his own, out at Bulwell. At the moment he's sleeping out there, on his work-bench. He used to sleep here with me, but we had a bit of a quarrel.'

His face had gone ugly behind the smile.

'Didn't we?' he said in a hard, mocking voice to his friend.

Becker merely shrugged, his mouth full of food.

It was getting late, and I got up to go.

'I'd like to come again,' I said impulsively. I felt changed and different. My old cautious self would never have spoken like that.

74

Kelvin stood up, full of grinning irritability, and led the way towards the door.

'Why not,' he said. 'See what happens.'

'All the best,' Becker called out as I was leaving the room.

At the doorway Kelvin seemed anxious to get rid of me, starting to close the door immediately. He poked his head out for a second in a comical fashion, looking up the empty street.

'Cheerio, then,' he said, drawing back.

The street was dark. There was a cold wind scraping through it, and the darkness seemed bristling and sinister, with no heart at the centre of it.

'When should I come?' I asked obstinately. It was like putting my foot in the door. The question irritated him.

'Don't know,' he said in a low voice. 'Don't want to force things. Anything can happen – don't like making arrangements. Don't believe in it.'

I saw that his face was lean under the beard. He looked drawn and tired, with a set face, as if the evening had exhausted him. He darted a wolfish look at me, and was about to shut the door, when I said:

'The old woman at my lodgings was quite excited about your visit. You certainly made an impression – you roused her curiosity all right.'

I had said this to delay the parting, wanting him to say something more conclusive, more definite. And I wanted to say something else myself that was more satisfactory. I felt angry and stupid because I couldn't.

'Did I?' he said looking pleased. He became more friendly at once. 'Yes, I said a few things to the old girl,' he chuckled. 'Why not? I believe in telling them all – tell everybody. I tell all sorts of people about myself. Tell 'em the whole story, everything. As much as they can understand, anyway. You have to judge how far you can go. I found I was getting nowhere just keeping it locked up in here.' He tapped his chest. 'That's no good. You only get bitter, storing it away like that. When you start telling all and sundry, you'd be amazed at the queer things that happen. Wonderful, sometimes.'

The vibrant note had crept into his voice again. Then he said 'Ah well,' and hung his head mournfully, a screwed-up smile on his face. His mood had changed abruptly. As he started closing the door again, he said, 'I'm always here, anyway.'

Turning away, I caught sight of his face for an instant in a shaft of light. He looked dejected, almost in despair. Jerking back suddenly, he slammed the door.

Chapter 7

I HEADED back into the heart of the city, walking swiftly and sightlessly, hardly conscious of walking at all. It was a long walk back, but the idea of catching a bus never occurred to me.

Going past a great block of government offices, I glanced up at the clock, high up on the cliff-wall. The time was so much earlier than I had expected – only eight-thirty – that I slowed down automatically. I could hardly believe it, and wondered if the clock was out of order. I had thought it was nearer ten or eleven.

My head felt full to bursting with thoughts. Something was churning inside me, and I exulted in everything. The gusty night was magnificent now, tearing at my clothes, rushing and blooming like a wild sea.

A few seconds later I had a moment of perfect lucidity, a wave of tremendous power and energy sweeping through me. It was like an enormous racing wave of understanding, and I felt the inevitable beauty of everything on the earth. At the same time I wanted to laugh out loud, and an urgent need of release sprang up in me. Going past the iron gates of the city hospital, I started to run. The thought flashed through me that pain was a mistake, disease, suffering; and the hospital became hideous to me, a place of cruelty and misery and error, more dreadful then the crucifixion.

I even looked down at my hands because they seemed so full of power. What could I do with such terrible hands?

I laughed out loud, trembling. It was a brief snort of

laughter, almost like a cough. Then I seemed to wake up and come back to normal. Everything looked ugly and safe and familiar, the world rotting away peacefully. I went into a snack bar for a cup of coffee.

'What an evening,' I told myself shakily, yet feeling very pleasant, no longer lonely. I tried to understand what had made me get up and leave so early, thinking I had been there for hours, when I was enjoying myself so much.

The thought of the evening pleased me. It was a real achievement for me, and now I didn't feel so utterly dependent on Stella. The girl pushed my cup across the counter and I smiled stupidly. 'Now I've got a foothold in this city,' I thought, taking pleasure in reminding myself. I felt proud and strong and happy.

A little later it occurred to me that I was attaching far too much importance to a first meeting. How did I know they liked me? What if they were mercilessly ridiculing me back there? What made me so optimistic about everything, so certain that something would come of it?

None of this reasoning affected me. I was curiously beyond logic, looking around with a calm eye, sipping the hot, greasy liquid. The brown counter was wet and glistening. It had a shiny chromium-plated rim. With the coffee running pleasantly down my throat, I let my gaze wander off along this rim.

A poor, elderly man was sitting at the other end of the counter, saying something in an indistinct, timid voice. I found myself looking at him. His round, narrow shoulders filled me with pity. He wore glasses, and a cap. His clothes were cheap and ill-fitting. I guessed from the way he held his body that he had known drudgery and insult for a long time. He was evidently the kind of man who never questions his fate or expects anything better from life. His very servility, instead of making me contemptuous, wounded and humbled me, and without understanding I became aware of the necessity of this world and the utter folly of revolt. I tried to picture this man as a baby, someone who had had a mother.

When he shuffled out through the door I watched the movements of his large, ugly boots on the bright red floor, keeping my eyes off his face. I didn't want him to see me staring and think I was passing judgement, though I was never further from that. Something urged me to run out and follow him, keep an eye on him, not let him out of my sight, because he was a sort of touchstone. Yet I sat there, gulping slowly at my coffee, with my optimistic mood ebbing away. Then I got up and returned to my lodgings, glad to see the old people again, glad of any human contact.

Though I wanted to go back to Kelvin's place the very next day, I resisted it, and kept on delaying, not wanting to appear too eager. And there was his behaviour at the door, when he had seemed anxious to get rid of me. If that was true, there would be no point in going back. I decided to wait another week, to give them time to make their minds up about me.

It was a bad week, because I had nowhere to go. I spent hours in the Castle grounds. Finally it became so bad, the time dragging so abominably, that I started setting little tasks for myself, studying plants, and even blades of grass, allotting myself a certain time for each task.

But the Public Library was my chief refuge, that and the Reading Room. I sat there for whole days at a time, only coming out for food and air.

Sunday was a special little nightmare set apart, when everywhere was emptied of life. On weekdays there was the streets and the Library, and in the evening the cinemas beckoning me with their promise of dark warmth and oblivion. I kept away from the cinema, not so much through lack of money, but because I always found the world a more desolate place when I stumbled out again, dazed and blinking. All the waste and emptiness would sweep up and make an onslaught on me, choking me with nausea.

I preferred the streets. I had a passion for them, walking down countless back streets and alleys, peering into doorways, wandering under damp archways and bridges until my legs became too weak. I liked to explore the maze of passage-ways and narrow streets in the old quarter of the city. I often got lost there.

It was inevitable that my thoughts should swing back to Stella again, though I had tried to keep her out of my mind. As I walked I devised impossible schemes for meeting her, telling myself that all I wanted was to talk to her for a moment. Her failings were so unreal to me now, so insignificant, that I had difficulty in calling them up in my memory. I was like a man in prison who dreams about freedom as a state of bliss; I remembered only the good things about her.

When a note came from Kelvin, five days after my first

visit, it made me childishly happy. It said:

> 'I thought you might like to know that George, the
> one I told you about, is dropping in here on Sunday,
> so he tells me. I told him a bit about you – all I know,
> which isn't much. He'd like to meet you, he says. There
> you are, I leave it to you. I told him you might be here.
> Now I'll sit back and let things happen, like a Chinese
> boyo. How's things with you? Love, Jack.'

I was jolted by the word 'love' at the end of it, and
wondered if he had written it by mistake, or if it was a queer
sort of formality he was in the habit of using.

When I got to know him better, it was easier to understand.
One of his pet theories at this time was that it was possible
to 'emanate' love – I believe that was the word he used. He
loved words like that; they were characteristic of him. When
he said them he tasted them, then let them fall slowly from
his mouth, rolling up his eyes like Al Jolson and clasping his
stomach.

At about three on Sunday afternoon I arrived at his house.
It was a beautiful spring day. The street was in shadow
because of its high buildings. A gang of youths lingered in
the road, talking in loud, jeering voices. Then they drifted in
different directions, dispersing aimlessly.

The street door was unfastened and slightly open. I called
'Anybody home?' and started to go in.

There was low babble of conversation in the back living-
room. I heard fragments of heated, angry talk, and then they
fell silent, like conspirators, just before I entered the room.

81

Kelvin had his back to me. He sat on the end of his divan bed, drinking tea. Becker was there again, in the same chair, wearing the same clothes, and with his usual easy grin. It was uncanny, as though nothing had changed and no one had been anywhere since last time.

The other man I had never seen before, so I assumed he was George Meluish. He sat in the armchair I had used before, opposite Becker. I saw at once how thin and impoverished he was. His beard was square and broad, very coarse, trimmed carelessly. It clung to the sides of his face, giving him an unkempt, tramp-like look. He was frowning down at his lap, and this, together with his crouched, round-shouldered way of sitting, made it difficult to tell how old he was. But I thought he was probably no older than Becker, who was thirtyish. I kept looking at his hands. They were badly treated, raw and scarred, with square, splitting nails. They were like tools, crushed and blunted with manual work.

He had a large book on his lap which he was opening and shutting slowly, like a man unable to read, letting the pages flutter down. There was something moving in this, as I looked at him, and I thought of a down-and-out playing with a toy. The book looked incongruous in his workman's hands.

'I'll get another chair,' Becker said lazily. He lounged into the kitchen.

'When I got your note I was almost on my way here,' I said to Kelvin.

'Oh?' He went on drinking his tea. 'That's interesting.

82

You weren't surprised to hear from me, then?' His voice was rather cold and reserved.

'Well, yes. I didn't expect it.'

Becker carried in a kitchen chair which had been painted green.

'Like some tea?'

'Thanks very much.'

He nodded and looked around vaguely, his thick lips parted, giving his face a stupid, dreamy expression. Then he lounged off again, slowly and sluggishly.

'Fill the kettle up, Beck,' Kelvin shouted at his back, coming suddenly to life.

Something about him made me want to grin, He looked so neat and dapper sitting there, in newly-pressed worsted trousers and a lemon-yellow shirt. His queer, ugly face poked up strangely out of his bright fresh shirt. It was like a knotted root sticking out of a flower-bed. Looking at him, I thought of a goat decorated with primroses; the wily and cunning dressed in innocence. It looked altogether wrong and comical. He perched there, very much alive, like a renegade canary. He would sing when he was ready, not before.

Becker brought in two cups of tea, one for himself. He handed me one and winked.

'No sugar,' he drawled. 'You'll get used to it.'

'Why not bring the pot in, man?' Kelvin said. 'We don't want to keep going in there. . . . All right, I've got to go out for a wet,' but Becker was half way in the kitchen again.

'Go on, then,' Kelvin said.

He swung up his legs and stretched on his bed, lying on

his back, as if bored with everything. But his eyes were open, staring up at the ceiling, and once his face twitched around the mouth, as though he had been stung.

I had taken him for a big man, but I saw that his legs were thin, and he had small feet.

Becker had come in and placed the brown teapot on the table. Then he sat down, dull and inert.

I glanced over at Meluish, wishing he would speak. I wanted to know more about him, and I was curious about his voice. He still sat motionless, cramped and stiff, still opening the big book with an almost insolent, illiterate action, letting the leaves flutter back with their own weight. I sat in the room as an intruder, yet I felt strangely indifferent. It didn't matter. I guessed Meluish had been absorbed in this book before I arrived, perhaps reading aloud from it or discussing it or having an argument about it. Now he was interrupted. 'Perhaps he is waiting for me to go,' I thought, not caring. I sat there obstinately. The note from Kelvin lay in my pocket like a passport. I drank my tea in the lull, gulping it down nervously and hardly noticing what it was. It had been so much diluted with hot water that now it was almost tasteless.

Meluish leaned over and lowered his book to the floor, clumsily. It half-dropped from his fingers. He made a fumbling, scratching attempt to straighten the crumpled dust-jacket with his finger-tips, hanging awkwardly out of his chair and grunting. Then he gave it up and lurched to his feet.

'I'm a-goin',' he said dully, in a broad accent. He had

gone over to Kelvin's bed.

'Are you, George?' asked the other man, mockingly, squinting up into his face.

'Aye,' Meluish said. He stood there, tall, letting his arms dangle. His bony shoulders seemed permanently stooped, and when he had moved across the room he had hobbled, as though his feet were blistered. It was painful to watch.

'Elizabeth's comin', you see,' he said thickly. 'She might be theer now.' He jammed his hands into his jacket pockets and stared down, lumpish and wooden.

Kelvin smiled up at him as if amused.

'She might be theer,' Meluish repeated, in a louder voice. And Kelvin laughed.

'Only one way to find out, George,' he said.

His hands were behind his head as he lay there. He was a curious contrast to the other man, who wore a coarse suit made of some dark hairy material and looked like a tramp. Yet they were both of the same class. They needed few words to communicate with one another; something passed silently between them, beyond their speech. Finally the standing man turned aside as though satisfied.

'Aye,' he said.

He hesitated at the door for a second with his back to all of us.

'So long, then,' he mouthed, childishly, as though he had just learned to talk. Then he hobbled out. He looked in a bad way.

The outside door banged. When Kelvin heard that he suddenly sat up. 'Where's that bloody teapot?' he muttered, getting up and going to the table.

'What d'you make of him?' he asked me from where he stood, the teapot poised in mid-air.

'I like the look of him.' I was surprised by my own words. 'Where does he live, did you say?'

'Over some stables. The bloke who owns the place had some rubbish in it. George and me cleared it out and fixed it up, and he moved in. If you like we'll pay him a visit one of these days. He pays the owner five bob a week for it out of his dole money. Me, I wouldn't live in the dump if you paid me, I think it's a shocking place. But he says it's better than the Salvation Army, and he can paint all day long up there. D'you know what it is? Just the space between the ceiling and the roof – you have to climb up a ladder through a hole in the floor. I'd say myself it wasn't fit to keep a dog in. There you are, he's up there, like a bloody hermit. Never sees anybody to talk to for weeks at a stretch – that's why he can't speak properly. Bloody fact! When I first met him he was at a hostel, digging holes in the road for the Corporation. Then he got this craze about wanting to be a painter and went on the dole. Got himself registered as an out-of work artist.' He laughed, and looked across at Becker. 'It's a fact, isn't it?'

His friend nodded and smiled.

'I'll tell you something else,' he went on, growing excited. 'D'you know what he comes here for? The real reason?'

He paused. He was enjoying himself.

'To read that bleeding book of mine, that's what!' he roared, pointing at it on the floor.

Becker burst out laughing.

86

'It's true. He's been coming here for weeks reading it. He just parks himself and picks up where he left off last time. It's a text-book on the technique of oil-painting – bores me to tears. Technique of the old masters – all that junk. I bought it when I was at the art school. Old George soaks it up like blotting-paper; he can't get enough of it. If I made him a present of it, he'd never show his face near the place again. Once he had that bag of tricks and formulas up his ladder, you wouldn't budge him with dynamite. The sod, he'd never ever come down then!

'Christ knows what he does with himself, apart from painting. There's a cat he's got now, stinking the place out. . . . It strayed in from somewhere. Maybe he talks to that.'

He had got to his feet in his excitement. Now he sat down on the bed again, his eyes darting about. His face was rapt.

'I want to see what he's up to, or I'd *give* him the damn book,' he went on rapidly. 'He knows a lot about music – you wouldn't think it to look at him. A lot, compared to me, anyway. There's a fiddle hanging on the wall up there, thick with dust. I heard him have a scrape at it once. He can play all right. I think he wanted to be a professional once and started practising about six hours a night after work – went at it like a fanatic. But he's done too many labouring jobs. See his hands? He reckons he wants to paint pictures like Sibelius composes music. Landscapes. That's all he's interested in, landscape and still-life. No figures. He's onto something, I think. Only he's so bloody illiterate, such an ignorant bloke, he can't tell you. He's a fanatic; that's why he's on the wrong track. You can't tell him anything. He'll sit like a lump of wood and look at you. I gave him a pair of shoes once, and an old mac. He takes anything you offer him, carts it up his ladder, but he'll never let you in on what he's thinking.'

His speech flooded over me warmly; I felt charged with some of his own energy. His face was tinged slightly with malice and amusement, yet it still had a rapt look. As he spoke, jerking his bright yellow arms at us, he sounded half-angry, half-affectionate. I found myself being drawn to him as a source of crude life, warming to his vitality, to his comical battlefield of a face.

There was admiration in Becker's large dreamy eyes, when I looked at him, though he must have heard it all before. Being naturally indolent, he was content to sit and look, to be the audience, to admire and nod and encourage.

I could understand that. I wanted to start Kelvin off again myself, to see his face again. And I was curious about a lot of things now.

'Who's Elizabeth?' I said.

'What's that?' Kelvin ducked his face round as he was reaching for a book.

'George said that Elizabeth would be there – before he went out. Who's she – his girl?'

He shrugged, keeping his face half-turned away.

'They're getting married. She's German; works at the mental hospital . . . nurse. . . . Bloody fool! He came round here one day – listen to this – and asked me to write a letter for him. He can't write much more than his own name. "Write and tell her I'm breaking off the engagement," he

88

said. "Don't you think that's best?" he asked me, "now I'm going to be a painter?" Probably he'd been reading about one of the old masters or some bloody thing, I don't know, but I agreed that it was the best way. You know me, Beck; I always believe in agreeing with people! I wrote his letter, we sent it straight off, and the next thing I knew, she turned up here and gave me a lecture on his lack of character! "Why couldn't he tell me himself?" she wanted to know. I don't like her, never did; she gives me the creeps somehow – a real house-frau. Never smiles, grim as hell. The sort of woman you can't imagine yourself in bed with. . . . Christ knows what he told her eventually, but there you are; they're getting married. And where d'you think they're going to live? – In that bloody loft of his!'

He stared at me contemptuously, as if I were Meluish. His face now was open and uncouth, and the common brutality of soldiers and factory workers mixed into his words. He had been in the army. His voice took on a harsh steeliness, a mechanical, meaningless sort of brutality. He fell into the way of it because he had used it so often, and I had heard so much myself that I took it for granted, disregarded it. I guessed that he was using it deliberately now, preferring it to the cultural lisping he must have met with at the art school.

And Becker was uncouth in a different way, more slow-moving and rustic and unassertive. I had never heard him swear, though his home was working-class and his father some kind of tradesman.

Being younger I was less brutalized than either of them, so that I made allowances, but not in a superior way. I envied them, and tried instinctively to blunt my sensitivity, to make myself more callous. I envied Becker's rather stupid cheerfulness, and Kelvin's unfeeling single-mindedness, his way of ploughing forward blind and direct.

I found myself imitating them because I wanted them to like me. It seemed important to have their acceptance. If I could, I wanted to have the comradeship of these men. I liked them. Little things were unimportant. I would submerge the little differences and be like them, I told myself; I was sick of being isolated. In one way I felt superior, more sensitive, able to create a world out of myself; yet I felt inferior and out of it, less of a man, when we were all together. My strength, I knew, lay in my difference to them, and I should have been proud of this difference. That had always been my way. But it was bad to be so isolated. Something perverse and dangerous wanted it to remain so, something I half-hated and tried to struggle against. Yet it always won.

Now I had a real chance, I thought. I was among these men, who themselves had a kind of stigma on them, and they were all men of my own class. It was something I had dreamed of.

Chapter 8

THERE was another question I wanted to ask.

'How did you come to meet him?' I said curiously.

'Who – George?'

'Yes.'

It was beginning to get dark. A sort of mauve light had gathered in the room, giving it a soft mystery. I felt mellow and content, perhaps richer than I had ever felt. Even now I was hugging my difference to myself, but I liked the company of these two men. I sat glad with hope and warmth among them.

Kelvin seemed pleased by my question.

'In the army, before the war,' he said readily. He was gay about the eyes, and then his face went straight. 'I was in India – I met him in Calcutta, when we were both at the same camp. He was a wild man out there, mad as a hatter. Now he's calmed down a lot – altogether different in a way. He used to grab a bloody great knife in the cookhouse and chase after the wild dogs that hung about round there, howling their heads off because they were starving. When we got to be mates, everybody used to say to me, "Is that your pal – the looney?" Then the war broke out and I lost track of him. He was taken prisoner in France, apparently – then he escaped and got back here somehow. They say when he came off the boat at Liverpool he had hair all over his face, like an ape. But he was a wild man before that.'

'I can imagine it.'

'This is the funny part. After the war he couldn't stick the life. He'd changed. All he'd joined up for, anyway, was to get away from his old man, who lies around drunk all day, so I understand.'

'He got it into his head one day that he wanted to play the violin. And, being George, that meant doing it all the time – nothing else. So he just sat about and thought about it, staring at the ground. He never turned up for parades, got slung into the glasshouse and Christ knows what. None of it made any difference; George was listening to violins. When they tackled him about it, he gave them daft answers. They even hauled in the old psychiatrist and gave him a going over. He baffled them all, so they threw him out. Discharged – mentally defective!'

He exploded with laughter, rocking backwards and forwards, braying like a mule. Becker became infected and joined in, his shoulders heaving, and then it reached me, like a wave washing round the room. It was impossible to escape.

'Isn't that typical!' Kelvin spluttered. Then he calmed down abruptly and sat sadly shaking his head.

'I don't know. I don't know,' he said.

For a time Becker still sat in his role of audience and admirer, while his friend talked on. Then he got up and wandered about languidly, pouring out more tea, picking up a book and glancing at it without interest. I wondered what *his* story was, and Kelvin's.

'Come and see the paintings,' Kelvin said suddenly, breaking off. He got to his feet. 'They're not all here, I've got some upstairs. These'll give you an idea, though.'

He seemed strangely awkward and off-hand. It was obvious that he was vulnerable and sensitive about his work, ill at ease now that a stranger was about to look at it. But he had suggested it. All he had told me had only made me more curious. He led the way, and I followed him along the dim passage.

'You coming, Beck?' he called at once, in a hard, tight voice, pausing before another door.

Then he went in. He left the door open, and a minute or two later Becker ambled through it, his hands in his pockets.

'Shut the door; I should,' Kelvin told him nervously. 'You can't turn round with three people in this box.'

He was very tense. He came and stood by my side while I gazed around in wonder. There seemed a flame of colour running over the walls, mainly yellow. Gradually I began to make things out, feeling the strain of the other man as he waited for me to speak. He stood at my elbow in bitter silence, as though fuming inside himself for suggesting that I should look.

'He's afraid I'm going to pass judgement on him; that's why he's so nervous,' I thought. It annoyed me because he had so entirely misunderstood me, thinking that. Why wasn't he able to tell instinctively that I would never pass judgement on a man's work? He was a fool to misunderstand.

We were in the front room. There was a choking smell of soot, and an odour of damp. A dingy, greyish pair of curtains were drawn over the window; through a chink I could see the street. The naked electric bulb shone down on my head.

It had bewildered me for a moment, coming without warning upon such a blaze of colour. The room was full of paintings, all oils, some of them framed and hung, others merely lodged against the walls, or on the mantelpiece. There was no sign of an easel; no materials were lying about, no brushes or tubes.

Every painting was boldly done, harsh with strength, the figures all made crudely simple, for maximum impact and strength. One or two figures were taut and compact, but the others were wooden. The colour was similar, rich and hot and very strident, laid on in broad slabs. There was a lack of fine feeling in it all, a monotony. Nothing was tepid or hinted.

'It gives you a jolt,' I said, to say something, and I put awe into my voice.

Kelvin hung his head as though dejected and shuffled his feet. He grimaced. Now he was here, the whole spectacle seemed to disgust him.

'I suppose so,' he muttered finally, with an almost theatrical misery. Then he cursed: 'Bloody junk, piles of junk! Who wants it now I've done it? What's the point? There's another roomful upstairs, as much again as this. Who wants the stuff?'

He slouched over to the corner for a piece of rag.

'It gives me a queer feeling when I look at it,' he said, more quietly.

He bent down at my side to examine a small canvas he had forgotten, wiping the dust off with his rag. Becker had found a space of wall near the fireplace, and he leaned back on it, propped up, gazing around vaguely, like a visitor waiting for a guide.

I liked best a large painting of a pregnant woman, a nude, the hands clasped over the belly, the back slightly bent. It glowed out, the warm orange-yellow colour tinged faintly with green. Probably it had been done on a green ground. The figure itself had a wooden, squat ugliness, not unattractive, like a piece of sculpture, rather lifeless in its drawing. But the attitude gave it a certain artless look which I found moving; and there was this greenish-gold efflorescence, this sun-and-fields colour, which he had got in some of the other paintings.

'The sun's in them,' I said. 'That's what they make me think of. Sun and ploughed earth.' I told him only the good things.

He shrugged, feigning indifference. I saw that he was pleased.

'Well, there they are. You can say you've seen Kelvin's masterpieces. I don't suppose I'll do any more; it was a phase I had to pass through. To keep on painting when you've said your say is sheer lunacy. I've said mine. That's it; I'm not interested now. It doesn't concern me, whether they're masterpieces or worthless junk. They're just coloured canvas, and I did it. I'm beyond it now, I don't need to paint.'

He spoke with such a lack of enthusiasm, frowning, his voice carrying an edge of bitterness, that I didn't know what to make of his statement. I wondered if he had perhaps been ridiculed for his work a good many times before, until he

95

had adopted this attitude as a defence, to ward off adverse criticism in advance. Really he was proud of his paintings, I thought, and that made him touchy. They were so naked, so out in the open, hanging up there. It like inviting attack on your self-respect and vanity.

We went back in single file to the living-room, in a comical silence. The room had a cold, empty look in the electric light. I sat glumly, gazing at the floor, unable to recapture the glad feelings I had known during the afternoon. I struggled with a grey futility which kept rising up inside me like a fog. Kelvin had gone out to make more tea.

'Have you got a job, Keith, or not?' I asked Becker.

He shifted about in his seat, then moved his head, as though the words refused to come out. He looked annoyed, yet a friendly voice came out of him.

'I've got *something*, and they pay me for it,' he said humorously. 'I don't know what you'd call it. I'm supposed to be training to be a cinema manager. You'll see me there most days, in the foyer of the Roxy, out at Ashfield. All I have to do is stand there and nod, beam at the right moments, and watch the morons stagger in and out.'

'Sounds a bit monotonous. Don't you do anything else?'

'That's all so far, anyway. I've only been there a week. It's touch and go whether I can stick it another week.'

He grinned across ruefully, rubbing his head like a baby.

'I can see them taking me away from there in a straitjacket!' he said.

'Serves you right, serves you right!' bawled Kelvin from the kitchen.

'What d'you mean?'

'What I say. Why accept such a foul job? Why have their stinking jobs at all?'

Becker made a sarcastic nod sideways with his head, as he looked at me.

'What's the alternative?' he called.

There was no answer.

'What's the answer?' he called again.

'Be like me!' Kelvin shouted at the top of his voice.

Becker looked amused.

'Like you? You sponge off me – me and your brother, when he's amiable.'

'Well, there you are, then. There's your answer.'

Kelvin had just carried in the tray, with fresh tea. He grinned cheekily at me.

'I don't get it,' Becker drawled, looking at him.

'Easy. *You* find somebody to sponge off.'

'Listen to him,' Becker said sarcastically, turning to me. 'Just because he's gifted that way, he thinks we all are.'

'Okay, if you're so fastidious, watch the morons going in and out,' Kelvin said sourly. He was being deliberately insulting, on principle.

He handed me a cup of tea.

'Get your tea, Beck,' he told his friend, who sat against the table. 'Somebody try and bring some sugar next time, will you?'

I started to sip my tea, and ended up gulping it down swiftly as usual. It was the tenseness and excitement and strangeness, the stimulation of these two men, making me unconscious of what I was doing. As I reached forward and put my empty cup on the table, Kelvin said casually, 'You must be in a state, drinking it back like that.'

I laughed awkwardly, caught out. 'I didn't notice,' I confessed, feeling my face go red.

'You were worse than that, last time you came here,' he went on calmly. 'You're in a state, you are! I'd say you were burning yourself up with something. We noticed it last time; it stood out a mile. When I followed you from the bus, as well, I noticed it. Like a cat on hot bricks. You want to take it easy. Stop lashing about in here.' He patted his chest. 'I used to be like that, just like that – didn't I?' He had asked Becker, not expecting an answer. His friend merely grinned.

I was grateful for his last remark; it let me out. I no longer felt cornered. Yet I watched him nervously, not wanting any more of that. It was curious how his few words had made me suffer and withdraw, isolated and taut with pride again; though he had told me nothing I didn't already know. I cursed him because he had confirmed it.

It was ten and I got to my feet reluctantly. I didn't want to go, I had said nothing I really wanted to say. Becker rose, too, and stretched out his arms, letting his head hang like Christ on the cross. Then he let out a huge yawn.

'I'll come with you,' he said, 'or I'll be missing the last bus.' To Kelvin he said: 'Don't know when I'll be round again, Jack – can't say for sure when it's my night off. Maybe Thursday. But I'll be here Sunday afternoon, for certain.'

Kelvin trailed after us to the door. He seemed restless.

'I'm always here,' he said in a doleful voice.

He was just as I had seen him last time, when I had left him. He looked miserable, and sidled about in a queer manner.

'I'm waiting for a beautiful woman to find out where I live,' he added in a half-hearted attempt to be cheerful. He grinned with his large mongrel's teeth, his eyes unhappy, shutting the door on us.

We walked steadily through the dark streets, now strangely hushed and free from traffic, beautiful in their quietness, with the shrouded, flanking houses. Nearly all the life of the streets had receded now, recoiled to lie behind doors and windows, in secrecy, and now there was a free way for us. I felt the withdrawal on all sides along the clear, darkened avenues. There was a sense of great peace and relief. The light of countless stars gathered in the sky. The air was soft and warm, lapping against my face.

'Which way do you go now?' Becker said, when I hesitated at a corner. His face was pleasant and loutish, his voice friendly.

'It doesn't matter,' I answered. 'I don't want to go in yet; I feel like walking. Which way is the bus station? D'you get your bus by the market.'

'That's it. Over here.'

We crossed a wide boulevard and headed downhill, towards the railway sounds. Two drunks swayed by, thumping each other on the back.

'Kelvin's certainly got a personality,' I said. 'He's alive. I didn't want to come away.'

'No.'

Becker looked at me, his flat, long face suddenly serious. He laughed low in his throat, as if the night had muted him.

'He affects me like that,' he said. 'I can sit there for hours listening to him. He's got something, I don't know what it is.' He was using words in a way oddly reminiscent of his friend. He frowned thoughtfully as he let his long legs carry him along. 'Whatever it is, it's something I want. I must do, or why should I keep coming back for more? Yes, he's alive, as you say. I don't take too much notice of what he says. Doesn't matter to me. Ideas, theories, don't interest me much. Jack feeds on them, gets himself all ravelled up in 'em. He's always got half a dozen ideas churning and pounding away, and new theories about life. I just like to watch him and hear him.'

He looked at me half-sheepishly, staring into my face and saying nothing, until I began to feel uncomfortable. Then broke out quietly and simply, 'He's the one, though – not me. I daresay you've noticed.'

I had grown more and more pleased with the man as he had been speaking; and it was a surprise. It was so unexpected, and I had under-estimated him badly. I felt an intense desire to speak to him about a lot of things which could not have been said before both of them. They were things which his simple voice had recreated in me, if I could muster the courage to say them. But we had reached the bus station. Seeing him with a preoccupied face as he looked about made me falter. Then he found he had ten minutes to wait, so we stood near the sheer red wall of the Ashfield bus, standing there in silence.

'He's more alive than his paintings, if you ask me,' I blurted out, saying anything in order to begin. 'I like him a lot though. I'd say he was a sort of leader; he'll draw people to him because he's alive and kicking. It's such a rare quality. Maybe somebody else will come along then, when he's brought a few of us together. I like him best like that, anyway – I think that makes him happiest, when he's on with his act, bringing us to life . . . not when he's being an artist. That's not for him, he won't be happy in that. I don't mean he's not an artist – no – but he should work with people, I think.'

Becker was looking at me happily, his mouth hanging open a little as he listened with great attentiveness.

'You're right, you're right,' he said warmly, and put his big hand on my shoulder. 'Yes, that's his role; you're right! I can see it now, he ought to be more like that. Of course! It's his role!' And he stared at me wide-eyed, smiling broadly. His pale eyes shone. I had never seen him so roused.

The bus roared suddenly into life, all its glass shivering. Turning to look, we found it full and about to move off. Becker had stepped back a few paces in his excitement, so that he was not so near. He loped over and climbed on just as it started to move. He waved his arm in my direction, standing on the step, making a broad gesture as though he were an American plainsman. That was his Walt Whitman wave. I saw him swaying unsteadily towards a seat as the bus rumbled away. Then it swung out of sight.

Chapter 9

Now that I felt partly accepted by them, I began calling at Hyson Terrace more often, sometimes two or three times a week, and always on Sundays, when they were both there. I was glad of a place to go, and I went also to see what would happen next, and to be able to laugh.

Kelvin's way of life fascinated me, though I was mystified by a lot of things. I asked myself if it was his own house and where he got his money from, for food and so on. It seemed a triumph, his freedom and independence, and I wanted to know how he had done it.

One day I went to his house quite early in the morning. It was about nine-thirty. I had come across a water-colour I had been carrying about in the bottom of my suitcase, rolled up and forgotten, and decided to show it to him. It was just an impulse; I wanted to see his reactions.

It was the first time I had arrived so early. Before it had always been in the afternoon or evening. He groped at the door, fumbling with the lock, taking a long time to open it. Then he peered round the edge of it, his eyes bleary and suspicious. He was still buttoning up his clothes.

'Oh, it's you. *Entrez.*'

'I didn't mean to get you out of bed,' I said. 'I'll come again later on if you like. Only I brought this to show you.'

'What is it?'

'A water-colour. Undiscovered masterpiece.'

'Good, good. No, I wasn't asleep, I was writing poems in

bed. Wonderful! Inspired, I was. Wrote reams of stuff.'

I followed him into the room. He wore slippers, and was pushing his yellow shirt into the top of his trousers, sliding in his hands as he shambled along.

'Wrote twenty,' he mumbled.

'Twenty?'

I thought he was joking. He had squatted down on the bed among a heap of papers, scratching his head and yawning.

'Here they are. This lot. Poured out of me this morning, so I just let it. Don't know what it's about, haven't read it myself yet. Read some if you like – here.'

Still scribbling on a sheet of foolscap with a ball pen, he reached over with his free hand and grabbed a pile of loose paper, holding it out to me.

'See if you can make head or tail of it,' he said. He grinned cheerily with the fangs and gaps of his teeth. 'Not that it matters. I felt wonderful when it was happening. Soon as I opened my eyes it started coming – must have been about five. I said out loud, "Christ, wait a minute, let me get some paper," – as if I was talking to somebody. What d'you think of that? Don't you think that's wonderful?'

I looked up quickly, smiling, to see if he was serious. Was this a cunning move of his to forestall any criticism? But it was obvious that he didn't care what I thought. When I examined the sheets of paper I found I could only read an odd word here and there. They bristled with exclamation marks; and that was all I could make out, apart from one or two obscene phrases. It seemed impossible for anyone to decipher that scribble.

'I can't read your writing,' I said, 'Why don't you copy them all out later?'

'Doesn't matter. See how I feel. . . . Who wants to copy things when you can be creating them? I'm in love, you see; that's what did it. Love. Wonderful, isn't it? The world, I mean. I love everything. I *am* everything. I am. I'm speechless because everything's so beautiful. It's all there on that paper and you can't read it, and neither can I. Nobody can read it, and you can't tell 'em. You just know or you don't. I know. Can't you see how amazing it is, me writing it and then neither of us being able to read it? It's perfect! Perfect! It's always been the same, and it always will be.'

He had begun calmly enough, talking as though it were a joke. I thought he was improvising to amuse us both; it was like an impersonation of himself. But now he had inspired himself. His eyes glittered and he couldn't sit still. He felt he had stumbled on a vital truth which cried out to be expressed. He had become a prophet, a mystic, and that made him very happy. Yet he nearly always ended by being too dramatic, and then it was comical. Like all buffoons, he uttered words of wisdom and revelation despite himself, amazed and delighted. I followed him with my eyes, admiringly, simply because he was such a dynamo of energy. And I asked myself suddenly if I kept visiting him because I expected him to lead me someone else. It was the first time this thought had entered my mind so clearly.

When I saw an opening I asked him quickly if George Meluish had been to see him again. But he was still full of himself and brushed it aside.

104

'Can you give me his address?' I persisted. 'I thought I might walk round there one day. You've made me keen to meet him,' I added cunningly, to flatter his vanity.

He made an irritable movement of the hands, waving my words away. He was impatient to get on with his own story. But he told me the name of the street; it was Chapel Street.

'You'll find his place at the top of the street,' he said testily.

Something stubborn in me made me say: 'Is that far from here?'

'No, no. Go past the Grand on the bus for about a mile, then get off outside a brewery. It's a back street near there.'

'Thanks,' I said.

Kelvin cast about to get started again. I had thrown him off his subject. Then his eyes grew smaller and beady, and he launched into a disjointed tale about a girl named June, and the effect she always had on him.

'Is she behind these poems?' I asked jokingly, not realizing it was the truth.

'Of course!' he cried, in almost a petulant voice. He was eager to tell me. 'I bumped into her the other day in the street, by accident – I know her to talk to. She's a dentist's receptionist – You know the type. Awfully nice – oh, awfully, awfully! Underneath that manner, though, she's quite a nice kid. The trouble is, nobody's touched her; she's unconscious of her sex; looks at you with big innocent eyes. Pure as driven snow – hasn't had the bloom knocked off yet.

'It was queer how I met her – the first time. Cyril Cooke – the one you haven't met, the joiner – got himself the job

105

of decorating the surgery, doing a bit of repair work on the window-frames, and so forth. It's all part of his job; he tackles pretty well anything to keep independent, keep the business on its feet. The point is, he asked me to give him a hand with this particular job and share the profit. . . .

'We got quite friendly with this girl. She'd drift up and start chatting, quite intelligent. When she dropped a remark one day about not having any beliefs, feeling the lack of a religion – naturally, I pricked my ears up. And naturally Jack Klevin tells her all about himself, there and then, on the spot. Cyril said to me afterwards, "D'you think she took it in, what you told her about civilization being in decline, every man for himself, and all that stuff? What can she know about life, to absorb that lot?" He always tells me that; but why be cautious? I don't get the point. What's there to lose? Tell everybody, I say.'

He busied himself about the room, talking continuously as he opened the door of a tall cupboard against the window and thrust his arm into the recess, feeling about for whatever he wanted. His hand came out clutching a huge packet of cereal, which he threw on the table. Then his hand plunged in again, this time emerging with a shallow white dish.

'I'm going to paint her portrait,' he said unexpectedly. He had tried to sound casual and keep the brightness out of his voice.

'June's portrait?'

He came out of the kitchen carrying a milk-bottle and a tablespoon.

'Well, they all go for it – romantic stuff! I only have to

suggest that; it always works. Easy. I just get a canvas or a piece of cardboard, get some brushes in my fist, and fool about. Gives me a chance to talk and have a good look. And they get used to me. Now and then I let out a suitable curse or two and screw up my face like Lautrec. You know – the suffering act! They love it. Or a bit of temperament; I fly off the handle, give 'em their money's worth. They either go goggle-eyed or pretend not to notice . . .'

'When is she coming?'

'I couldn't get her to say. . . . She'll come, though. They always do. Can't resist the flattery. . . . She'll be here.'

He made a wry face, looking thoughtfully at me. Then all his enthusiasm seemed to run out of him, and he became sad, deflated, baffled.

'Expect it'll turn out like the others. . . . I don't know. These "nice" girls who don't know what it's for – can you see her? Yet I always get tangled up with these sweet virginal types, and every time I end up scaring 'em off. Mention sex and they look at you like the Loch Ness Monster. Then they're off like the bunny rabbit. Ah, what's the use? A woman, that's what Jack Kelvin wants. A woman, with breasts and thighs and buttocks. An animal! That's his prayer, the poor devil. Here's me getting mixed up with souls again – virgin souls. Who wants a soul-mate, anyway? I'm my own soul-mate. Women and souls don't mix. Or if they do, it's a weird sort of stew. You don't know what you're grabbing hold of any more. Why can't I meet a woman like that wife of Maillol? When they asked him who was the model for his beautiful figures, he told them she was in the kitchen getting the dinner. His wife! Ah, they had the right ideas. And old Renoir. With his penis, he said, when they asked him how he painted. If I say that to June she'll run from here to Manchester.'

He sat at the table, hunched over his bowl of cereal, half-turned away from me.

'Still,' he mumbled, 'we'll see what happens, I suppose.'

His back had a bleak look. I did not care to see him like that. To cheer him up I mentioned Stella, and my own predicament, though it had become a little remote to me. I knew, from my enjoyment of his misfortunes, how good it was sometimes to hear of another man's problems.

'God strewth!' he said, and jerked round in his chair to look at me, 'not another one! Don't tell me *you're* up to your neck in it with a married woman?'

I nearly laughed when I saw his face.

'Why, who else is there?' I said, chuckling. His voice sounded urgent with interest, and I was flattered. Yet he looked at me with such concern that I began to feel ridiculously proud of myself, as though I had done something unique and daring. 'Have I got somebody to keep me company?'

'Me!' he shouted, bellowing with laughter. 'I'm not going to tell you all about that now, it's too involved, too morbid. You'll be depressed. Well, I'm damned – another one! Would you believe it? Where is this *femme fatale* of yours? Not here?'

'Yes, she's here. That's what brought me up here, in a way.'

'Well, I'm buggered. And how's it going – or isn't it?'

'It isn't. She's finished with me, pretty well. Though I

haven't had it out with her finally. I came up here to do that. Either that or patch it up, one or the other.'

He shook his head over me like a despairing priest.

'You were a fool to get mixed up in it. You don't know what you're playing with. It's dangerous, that game. If you'll take my advice you won't go near the place, wherever it is.'

'Sounds like the voice of experience,' I said, grinning my defiance.

He must have been delighted with the opening I had given him, but he delayed.

He darted a shrewd look at me that was meant to be grim.

'The things I could tell you,' he said archly.

'What things?' I said, with too obvious a stupidity.

He grunted. Then he dropped his spoon with a clatter and dragged round his chair to face me, plunging into the story.

'I got in a proper state, I tell you, with Doreen. My God, what a state!' He winced, gritted his teeth, frowned, laughed, all in a few seconds, striding about the room. His arms thrashed about as he grew more excited.

'You know the Arboretum – the park?' he said. 'I used to lodge in a house behind there, before Cyril Cooke and me came here. And at the back of the house the landlady had a derelict summer-house affair that was slowly falling to bits. "How about your summer-house for a studio?" I said to the old girl. She told me that I could do what I wanted with it if I repaired it at my own expense. So rigged it up – Cyril helped me. Half the roof had slid off; you never saw such a mess. Anyway, we fixed it up and I installed myself. Of course this landlady used to boast to everybody who called that she had a real live artist down there in the summer-house, all alone; a strange young man, struggling, missing his meals – trust her to embroider it. And she had a married daughter named Doreen, whose husband was an engineer at the Post Office. Stolid type, nose in the newspaper, falling asleep in his chair, boring her to death, and impotent into the bargain. Poor old Stanley! What a state of affairs! Typical. There was this marvellous woman, young, full of life, not a scrap of romance in her life, no sex, no nothing – and there was Jack, stuck in the summer-house, full of romance and poetry, watching the landlady's daughter in the garden with his tongue hanging out!'

He turned and faced me with his face distorted, which made him half-urchin, half-satyr. What a pity he knows he is so alive! I thought, watching him in admiration. What a pity he knows what he is! It was his knowledge of himself which overbalanced him and made him a buffoon. He knew he was expected to be a dynamo, a star-turn. Even so, he was good to watch. He danced forward now, then slouched off to one side, the street-corner lout coming out in him suddenly, and flung himself into an armchair.

'She was a woman. My God – wasn't she! One day Stanley nearly caught us. I just happened to glance up through the window and catch sight of him wandering along the garden path. I've never moved so fast in my life. You know, I never could decide if he knew what was going on, or if he was just plain stupid. Doreen hardly had time to get her clothes straight before he was walking through the door. "Come and look at this painting of Jack's," she said in a flash and grabbed his arm, steering him over to one corner.

'Whether *he* knew or not, the landlady certainly did; I can tell you that. But for some reason she didn't give the game away. I think she felt sorry for her daughter and turned the blind eye so that Doreen could have a change from Stan. If you'd seen him, you'd know what I was ranting about. He looked like a rubber stamp . . . poor bugger. . . .

'When it came to the test, though, the bitch let me down,' he cried, wincing with anger. 'The radio, the car, the vacuum-cleaner – they pulled the other way too damned hard. I told her she'd be poor with me. Not that she needed telling. She couldn't bear to leave her gadgets, and at the last minute she found she couldn't bear to do the dirty on Stanley, because he was so helpless without her. Tell me the old, old story! Yet in a way I don't blame her . . . and he's a pitiful object . . .'

He broke off and glanced very quickly at me. Then he sighed, his face taking on a martyred expression. I thought of a clown on the cross.

'Isn't it silly?' he said and let out another sigh. 'Ah well.' He smiled self-consciously. He looked utterly weary and disgusted, and I struggled to find something to say to him, but failed.

Finally I said, 'I've brought this water-colour, if you'd like to see it.'

'Yes, let's have a look,' he said, brightening up.

We unrolled it on the table and he stood over it importantly, like a general planning a campaign. I was staring at it with

111

such interest myself, having forgotten what it looked like, that at first I didn't notice Kelvin shaking his head.

'What's all this black?' he said.

'Where?' I was on the defensive at once.

'Everywhere. All over it. Black lines. Shadows. Don't you know black's a bad mystic colour?'

I stared at him.

'A what?'

'A bad mystic colour,' he repeated sadly, with great patience. 'Oh, you're in a state, you are. Look at all this.'

Looking down, I began to see what he meant. His words had begun to work in me. When I had painted it, I thought it was a joyous composition. Now I saw sinister undertones and black question marks. It was odd. And I had to admit that compared with his paintings there was no bright colour in it, only sepias, greens and browns, earth colours, and that objectionable question-mark colour. Question marks were banned in his paintings. I imagined him sitting down to paint and saying to himself, 'Now then, shut your eyes and ears, forget. Don't be weak and make it gloomy, be strong and fiery. The world is old and corrupt – set it on fire!'

'This tells me more about you than anything you've told me about yourself,' he announced solemnly. 'Ah well, if you like that sort of thing, I suppose you might as well do it. But you're in a state. Inside you're like that picture. All black lines.'

'So's the world,' I said shortly, 'and I have to walk about it in it, I can't help noticing things.'

'World? What world?'

'There,' I said, pointing at the window. 'That one, rubbing its ugly face on the glass. Civilization.'

'You mean syphilization,' he said, uncovering his teeth in a grin. Then he gave me a venomous look. 'Why bother with it? You didn't make it, did you? I don't even notice it. This is the only world I'm interested in.' And he made the significant gesture again, tapping his chest profoundly.

I knew he was lying, but I pretended to agree. We had rolled up my water-colour again, and I sat holding it, feeling slightly ashamed of it. 'Kelvin is a fool, but he stumbles on things,' I thought, back in my isolation once more. The black was there, in the universe; that was the point I had tried to make. You had to incorporate it somehow come to terms with it.

'The thing is, I'd find it a bit lonely in my own world, all by myself,' I said vindictively. 'I think I should even get sick of being my own boss after a time.'

Jack Kelvin knew I was really saying, 'Don't badger me,' and it made him angry.

His lips curled.

'No, no, you don't understand me,' he cried. 'Look, how can I make it clear – I'll put it this way. You get initiated – if you don't understand this jargon, then I can't explain it – you get initiated into higher worlds, you become one with things. One. Unity. The path. You are the path, the path is you, and the path is the goal. See? There's really no goal – it's all the path. Ah, it's impossible to explain,' he fumed, exasperated by his own lack of language, and he sat down abruptly with twitching eyes. 'If you'd take a course of Zen

Buddhism it would make a lot of things clear to you,' he said, and stared hard at my face. 'I've got a book you could have; it's straightforward enough.'

'I see what you mean, but I don't know if I could read it,' I said, speaking the truth.

'Why – why?' he asked irritably.

'I've tried before. Something about it repels me. Perhaps it's because it's got the dust of ages on it, or just that I haven't got enough patience. What bit I did read I saw the wisdom of, but . . . I don't know. There didn't seem anything there that vitally concerned me. All spirit and no flesh, too abstract. I didn't like it, somehow. I didn't see where it fitted in, or that out there.' I had pointed at the window. 'Perhaps the trouble is that we can't wear someone else's truth now, not properly. We're too individualized, I'd say. We've gone too far now. A truth like that fits where it touches, and it's got a sort of graveyard smell.'

I saw that I was making him angry, but I went on.

'Perhaps each man's got to weave his own truth, out of a sort of living cloth – a cloth that's got the smell of our time in it. ... As I say, I read a few pages, and that was as far as I could get, somehow.'

'What did you read?' said Kelvin stonily, glaring at my head. I had turned my face away.

'I can't remember now. No, I can't remember.'

'Whatever it was, you obviously didn't grasp it,' the man snapped, unable to restrain himself. He jumped to his feet and darted across to the bookshelf. 'Look here, if I give you these – lend you them – will you have a go at them?' Not

114

waiting for my answer, he came across with three books. 'Read this one first, then this, and this last. Remember the order. If you'll do that, it'll give you an idea what I'm yapping on about. You keep misunderstanding me. You're on the wrong path; that's what you don't seem to realize. They're only small books. When you've read those you can have some more, if you're interested.'

It was clear to me now that the idea of the holy man, the *swami*, went really deep with him. How he would have loved to be one, decked out in naked dignity and importance, with his followers. My blasphemous talk would not be forgotten.

Glancing at the titles, I found that I had a book of the Rosicrucians, *The Third Order of the Rosy Cross*, a thin volume called *The Way of Inspiration*, by Rudolph Steiner, and Evelyn Underhill's *Life of the Spirit*.

'I'm going out now,' he said bluntly. He was pulling on his jacket. 'I'm meeting somebody in town to-day, a chap who's promised to introduce me to some evangelist bloke, a business man, who shares out his profits, and reckons he's seen the light. He gets down on the floor in his office, apparently; kneels down there and offers up a prayer, in the middle of dictating a letter, or whenever it occurs to him. Sounds interesting. He might be the backer I'm hoping for – never know. Soon see.'

At the door, as I was about to follow him out, he stopped and turned round.

'How you fixed?' he said, in a mocking voice. 'Manage half a crown?'

I fumbled in my pockets while he stood with one foot

in the street, holding the door open. I felt flustered and embarrassed by our new relationship, painfully aware of being at a disadvantage. For a few seconds I hated him, because he was flaunting his poverty in my face, making me feel inferior. I would rather have given half the money I had, to put us on an equal footing again.

'That's okay,' I mumbled, giving him three shillings, and he slouched off immediately, away from me.

'Cheerio, then,' he shouted. 'Think of me this afternoon, down on my knees!'

It was the first time I had seen him in the street. I noticed how incongruous he looked, slinking along close to the wall on the pavement. His shoulders were hunched up as though for protection, warding everything off, and this lift of his big shoulders gave him a slouch. His body dwindled down at the hips into thin legs and small goat's feet. On these delicate feet he balanced carefully, seeming to pick his way along. He looked so exposed and fugitive in the open street. 'Yet I have seen him prance,' I thought. Looking after him, I felt a stab of pity, as a woman might. He looked hopeless and babyish.

Chapter 10

I CALLED at Hyson Terrace again about three days later; this time in the early evening, as usual. I would think around something he had said, then decide that I wanted to talk to him about it, making this my excuse to go back there. I could easily have gone every day, but I lacked excuses. Also, my pride kept me away.

Before I knocked I heard a soft hum of conversation which seemed to come from the front room, his studio. It had an intimate sound. Then it ceased. There were some hurried movements, and a loud 'Excuse me!' in a voice I hardly recognised as Kelvin's.

The door partly opened, and Kelvin squirmed round it and stood on the step, closing the door again behind him. I watched his antics in bewilderment, standing on the pavement. He wore a paint-smeared artists' smock and a black beret, his hair tucked neatly up out of sight, so that I could see his ears. He looked now like one of his self-portraits, except that in these paintings he made his eyes much larger than they were, and gave his skin a ripe, golden colour.

He put a finger to his lips, his face wild and happy, like a boy about to get a first glimpse of the sea. The street was deserted, which was lucky; otherwise we should have had some curious lookers-on. He aimed an enormous wink at me, leaning forward from the waist. He looked like a music-hall imitation of an artist – he even had a brand new hog's hair brush in his hand.

'She's here!' he hissed, peering up the street, his lips

springing apart, leering. 'I'm painting her portrait – what a lark!'

I was still confused. 'You mean June?'

'I told you she'd come!' He backed into the house, rolling his eyes at me ecstatically, waving me away. He looked drunk with happiness.

'Er – shall I come tomorrow?' I said stupidly, in confusion.

'Yes, yes – anything!' he hissed, grinning madly. Then he was unable to delay any longer. He jumped back and slammed the door. I heard the sedate murmur of conversation start up again before I moved away.

The following Sunday, when I went again, Becker was there.

'How did it go?' I asked Kelvin, but he only shrugged, smiling mirthlessly, as if it were a bad joke.

'Want to see what I've painted?' he asked later. And we both trooped after him into the studio.

He had sketched in a soft semblance of a portrait, all in a soft, indefinite manner, soft blues and pinks, utterly unlike the other paintings. We stood before the large misty canvas. Then, for something to say, I mentioned this different manner.

'Well, that's how she is,' was his only answer.

On the way back to my lodgings, I said to Becker, 'Is Jack in love at last?'

He made a wry face. 'Have you seen this June of his?'

'No,' I said.

'He introduced me to her the other day. She's stupid. Dead from the neck up. Not that it's anything to do with me. You see – he'll come a cropper again; he always does. I can tell what he's up to already, trying to build it up into something wonderful. I can see him struggling to convince himself. He always does that. Then it falls through, and he ends up feeling bitter. Why he picks that type every time, beats me. It's a vicious circle.' He spoke humorously, yet with concern in his voice. I had never known him so much in earnest.

'What was Doreen like?' I asked him.

He glanced at me in surprise. 'Has he told you about her?' And he laughed shortly. 'He'll never get over that one. I never met her, mind you. None of us did. She haunts him, that one. As far as I can make out, she was the only one who really accepted him, with all his faults; and he can't get over it. He never stops telling me about it; he goes over it in detail, until I'm sick of it. He's started on you, has he?' He shook his head. 'I've lost track of all his girls. Doreen was the nearest he ever got, or ever will, as far as I can see. I thought he'd given up trying, but apparently he's on the merry-go-round again.'

Getting on the Ashfield bus he made his slow, open-handed wave again.

'So long, Lou,' he called, ducking inside as the engine roared into life and the whole bus shuddered, moving slowly away.

I walked through the streets, brooding on what he had said. His description of June, and Kelvin's unrequited love, and so on, I had thought pathetic and slightly ridiculous. Now he had gone, his words troubled me. They had resurrected Stella, and now I felt an intense desire to see her. It rose up in me painfully, as if Becker had been telling me my own story. I grew feverish with longing, wanting Stella to look at me, so that I should be in touch with something gentle. I felt crushed and lost, starved of tenderness. My lust had fallen away like a dead husk, and I was left with this simple need.

I walked along Shakespeare Street, then turned mechanically into the narrow cul-de-sac. The gardens in front of the house looked evil and dead, like miniature cemeteries, wretched bits of stone and weed.

Lying in bed, I drew a deep breath. My heart felt choked with dumb struggle. The schools were open now. I could carry out my original plan, and meet Stella. It would have to be next week, I told myself, because it was my last week of freedom. I had got a job through the labour exchange – some kind of routine clerical work at a builder's office. My money had nearly gone, and that had forced my hand. But I was far from being sorry. I had grown stale and indolent, and thought a job would anchor me. So I had gone for the interview and been accepted by a tough little white-haired man with pig-like eyes. 'Any good at figures?' he asked, and that was all he wanted to know.

The next day I went to the suburb where Stella lived. I asked at a newsagent's shop where the nearest school was.

St. George's Road, I should think,' the woman said

doubtfully, and I walked out feeling naked and guilty.

Finally I found the school, and stood there with half an hour to wait. I walked about nervously, trying not to look suspicious. I felt like a criminal, and the absurdity of my plan, now that I had come to put it into operation, made me want to find an excuse and run off. How should I know Stella's daughter? I had never even seen her. I stared desperately at the towering, raw-brick walls of the school, hearing a muffled drone of voices, then a loud female voice chanting something, and thought of Stella getting ready to leave her house and make her way here. The grim, respectable houses hemmed me in, as though I should not be allowed to escape.

At last a door banged open and children began trickling out; first in ones and twos, then a stream, then a gushing river. I was lost. Screwing up my courage I went over to a girl who stood against the green railings, swinging her satchel. She shrank away from me immediately and looked frightened.

'Do you know a girl called Valerie?' I asked in a cracked voice. 'Valerie Brandon?'

'No,' she whispered, and edged away, then ran off to join her friends.

I turned in a panic to another child, this time a boy whose round face was masked with pale freckles. 'Do you know Valerie Brandon? As she come out yet?' I babbled, and the boy shook his head, running off on his small fat legs. Then a tall girl at my elbow cried, 'There she is, look – with the blue satchel!'

Thoroughly unnerved, I started to follow her. I had gone about fifty yards, keeping her in sight from the other side of the street, when I saw Stella hurrying towards her from the opposite direction. She was holding a paper carrier-bag and her dark red handbag, both in the left hand. I went half blind with fear or nervousness. She might have been an utter stranger. It was worse now because of the letters. The fear was blowing inside me in great gusts. It knotted the blood round my heart; I felt strangled with fear, and my legs had gone watery and useless.

Somehow I forced myself across the road to intercept her, though I longed to escape. I had to keep telling myself, 'It's only for a few seconds!' Then she had almost reached me, and I could see her pale face as it registered the shock of recognition. After all, she had thought I was a hundred miles away.

'Good God – I'm going mad!' she gasped.

I gulped and tried to smile, my mouth trembling, not able to look at her face.

She had grasped her child's hand, a blonde girl of six or seven, with straight hair, cut in a sharp, tidy fringe, who seemed very quiet and intelligent. We went on in silence as I looked down at the child, still trying to control my mouth. I felt Stella staring fixedly at me in amazement.

'I haven't come out of the ground,' I managed to say. My face felt horribly strung with taut nerves. I was disgusted with it.

'You have!' Stella cried. 'Good God, Louis, I'm shaking like a leaf!'

'So am I,' I blurted out, grateful for what she had said.

My spirits rose at once, and the tension seemed to fall

away. I even grinned, beginning to enjoy the commotion I had aroused in her. We came to a main road and turned into it, and an almost continuous noise of passing traffic enveloped us.

Stella's face was more strained and tired-looking than I had remembered it, but her eyes, alive with nervous intensity, were still the same. I was giving her flickering sideways glances as we walked. Her thin mouth was still set grimly against the world, and her voice, coming from that mouth, startled me as it always did, because it was so warm and vibrant. Then I noticed the same mournful, tragic expression run into her eyes which had often angered me, because I knew she liked to nurse her unhappy feelings. Yet I had learnt to accept it. It was her most typical expression.

'Where are you, then? Not living here, surely?' she said tensely, turning her head in a sharp, jerky movement.

'Yes. I'm in lodgings here. I start work next week, I've got a job.'

'But why?' she exclaimed in astonishment. 'What on earth made you come? Didn't you get my last letter?' she seemed too astounded to be angry.

I nodded meekly.

'Yes, I got it, but I didn't understand it.'

'Don't be silly,' she said in amusement, yet pretending to be severe. By the way she spoke, I guessed that the mood in which she had written her letter had died and been forgotten, and now the whole thing was unreal.

'Who is he, Mummy?' asked the little girl suddenly. She was walking between us very quietly.

123

'An old friend, darling,' said Stella, looking at me sardonically.

Evidently she was still struggling to grasp this new situation, for she said now, 'D'you know, I can't think straight! It seems so incredible, you being here.'

I laughed. 'Are you still shaking like a leaf?' I said.

'No, I've stopped. Are you?'

'Not now,' I said happily. Yet I was still far too nervous to speak calmly, without a slight break in my voice.

Suddenly Stella halted. We all stood at the corner of the road.

'You can't come any further,' she said; 'it's not safe.'

'Am I still suspected?'

'Naturally!' she cried in mock astonishment.

I was looking at the fringes of her lashes. They were long and curled.

'I ought to send you away. There can't be anything now, while he suspects. I'm not going to risk anything; I told you that.'

'Send me away, then. I'll go,' I said perversely.

'Will you?' And her mood changed. Her look was tinged with wistfulness. 'You've come here, though,' she said.

'Do you want me to go?' I muttered.

'You devil!' she said softly, and laughed. Then in a grim, semi-tragic voice she added, 'You know me too well.'

There was a moment of silence, as she waited for me to speak. But I had nothing to say now. The child gazed up at me steadily, beginning to get bored. She began tugging mutely at her mother's sleeve.

'I'll have to go. It's not safe here,' said Stella. 'People know me, and they talk. Don't spring on me like this again, will you? And don't come here, please.'

'Do you want my address?'

'What is it?'

I told her.

'I must go now,' she said in a harassed voice. 'Come along, Valerie. Good-bye, Louis,' she said to me over her shoulder.

She gave all her attention to the busy main road. When they reached the other side she turned and waved, smiling. Then they moved quickly out of sight, down a narrow avenue set with trees.

Turning back to the city, I felt resolute and strong, glad to be alive. I had no desire to see her again. Afterwards, when I thought of her as I walked through the streets, feeling all the mongrel lusts calling furtively in the dark, I lusted after her again. But now I did not want her. It had been enough to look at her and have her look at me, to feel the soft look of a woman on me again, after all the dead and stony looks from strangers. I didn't want to see her again. She would never be mine. It was a relief to be walking away, knowing that I had deliberately undergone the ordeal of facing her. And now it was over. I had triumphed over my fears. And this knowledge filled me with generous thoughts about Stella. I told myself that it was only when I goaded her for having an intrigue with me that she became barbed and cruel.

People were coming out of work, thronging the streets. I walked quickly, exhilarated by the hurrying crowds, heading back into the city as if it had challenged me, as if I could subdue it, overthrow its buildings. I felt I had the power and could do it.

Then I found myself toying with the idea of going to see George Meluish. The idea excited me; it seemed full of daring and freedom. I strode along eagerly, changing direction a little, so that eventually I entered the big central square, passing the newspaper stand, and the man with his basket of anemones, on the town-hall steps.

I stood in a long queue for the bus. A miner was directly in front of me, returning from his shift, and still wearing his steel helmet. He was in his dirt. He looked weird and impressive among the city suits and dresses, like a man from another planet. The cool April sun broke free above us, shining bravely. The miner's helmet gleamed as he stood stiff and motionless. He was a tall, scrawny man, with big shoulders and a long, bony head. He stood like a rock.

The bus drew up and waited, throbbing, like an enormous animal. It gobbled up the queue, then set off heavily, swinging uphill to the left, past the Theatre Royal, with its pompous entrance pillars, speeding along the level stretch of Alfreton Road.

The conductor came up – a little chubby man, jovial and sweating – and I told him where I wanted. I sat against the vibrating window, gazing out, watching the streets become more and more squalid and industrial. The monstrous bulk of the gasometer towered up suddenly, covered in orange rust. Then I saw the conductor signalling to me. It was my stop.

From the main road, along which the bus disappeared,

I had to climb up at right-angles, the narrow street rising steeply for about a hundred yards. Then it flattened out abruptly and stretched on into the distance, in two dismal rows of terraced houses. It reminded me of Birmingham.

Chapel Street was an opening to the right, on the last few yards of the hill. It was very narrow, barely wide enough for a lorry, with tiny cobbled sidewalks. It had no houses. There were two rows of buildings, sheds and garages and workshops, of varying heights and sizes, and at the far end I could see a bombed and gutted chapel. I walked past the back entrance of a dairy. Two men were inside, working in dense steam. They wore rubber boots and aprons and were manhandling churns and steel crates, the pitted concrete floor puddled with dirty milk. Then I saw the sign that Kelvin had told me to look for: Taylor and Sons, Hauliers, painted in red letters across the double doors of a large wooden structure. Above this was a narrow door, set high up, beneath a wooden frame which jutted out into space, a sort of hoist. Apparently sacks had been swung through that door. Now Meluish lived behind it. But I had to go around the side somewhere.

I found a gate in the wall, lower down, and entered a cobbled yard behind a row of slums. It was familiar to me. There was the iron pipe of the water-tap sticking up from the sunken cobbles, the surrounding ashbins and washhouses and lavatories, and tiny patches of dirt fenced off with matchwood, serving as gardens. It struck vivid chords in me, as though I were revisiting the scenes of my own childhood. I was very curious to meet this man; I did not feel I had really met him. He flitted through my mind like a phantom.

127

Kelvin had told me to cross this yard and enter the garage at the side. I saw this door. It was partly open. There was a queer silence everywhere, and my feet clumped loudly on the worn stones. I felt watched, like a trespasser.

The place was empty and very dim, light filtering through cracks in the walls and doors. It had no windows. The earth floor had a layer of fine coal-dust. There were broad tyre-marks, and a spreading puddle of oil. Near the back, against one wall, I could see the ladder, rising up vertically to a square hatch in the ceiling. There was no sound. I stood for a few seconds, gripped by the darkness and silence. Going to the foot of the ladder, I saw that the hatch was swung back, and called up through the square hole, 'Are you there?'

I heard a movement directly over my head, and heavy footsteps. Meluish's face appeared, framed by the hole, hanging over me upside down and peering into the gloom.

'Who's tha'?' he said loudly.

'It's me. Lou. Can I come up, George?'

There was an uncanny silence, and I waited while he thought out what I had said.

'Oh ah,' he said at last. ''Ow are yer! Aye that's right, come through th' 'ole.'

I climbed up self-consciously, expecting to feel ridiculous as my head and shoulders rose into sight, in the middle of his floor. But he had moved away from the opening and even had his back to me. As I clambered out I saw that he was painting, standing before an easel. There was a strange hush about the place, as there had been in the yard below. Life seemed a long way off, a harshness. There was no place for life in this stillness. I felt extraordinarily quiet. It had something to do with the district, being isolated from traffic, and something to do with the sun setting. I felt that nothing mattered.

Meluish's face was ruddy and transfigured as the light caught his face and beard. It was a strange time to see his place because the dying sun had turned it into a chapel. There were two smeared windows, one in each outside wall, set in the whitewashed bricks. A hardboard partition ran across, dividing the space in two, with an opening cut crudely in the centre and hung with a blanket, to serve as a doorway. I assumed that he had a bed on the other side. Where I stood, there was only a chair, a marble wash-stand with a few books, and his small paintings littered about. These paintings were curiously alike. Nearly all of them were of the same table-top, with one or two bottles standing, bereft of colour and drama, like poor people. I stared at them, not knowing why, until I realized how grave and weightless they were. They all had this humility, and the pallor of slum children. I was struck by their pathos.

I noticed a jagged hole high up in the partition which Meluish had made with a hammer in a fit of rage, when they had erected it. Kelvin had told me this.

'I'll be with yer, soon as I've done this bit,' Meluish said now, in his heavy way. 'Then we'll 'ave a talk, shall us?'

'There's no hurry,' I said, and went across to him. He had given me a chance to look at his work. I felt perfectly at ease with the man, though I doubted if I should be able to talk to him. But it was unimportant.

129

"Ow are yer, anyway?' he said thickly, out of his absorption. He was making an effort to be friendly, but I knew he had no desire to speak. He was absent. He stood painting an apple and a wine-bottle from life; they were arranged on the perforated seat of a folding chair in front of him.

'Not too bad,' I answered. Watching him lulled me. I felt drowsy and indifferent. He was daubing at a bit of plywood, making slow, stiff dabs at it with no perceptible effect. I marvelled at his patience and utter absorption. This painting was much more precise than his others. It looked like a Chardin. It looked so accurate and finished the silhouettes all corresponding, that I failed to see what he was doing, what there was left to do. Still he went on, the sun glowing magnificently through the window, bathing his neck and shoulders and one half of his face, while he touched at the sloping shoulders of the bottle, dabbing gently and firmly, then lifting his brush and looking forward, not moving his head. I stood fascinated. I had never seen a painter working before. It was like watching a ritual.

I realized that his was a monastic art. Looking at him, I thought: 'There is a deep unconscious desire to see one or two objects very clearly; and it shows itself in odd places, this desire. Here it is now. It is as though we must learn again what is in the world. Small, ignored things are the most important, though we shall never learn them all. It is a joy to learn.'

'The light's goin',' Meluish said, putting down his brush at last. 'I'd better pack up.' Then he roared out: 'Pack up,

George, me lad – pack up! Will-yer-bloody-well-pack-up!'

I had to laugh. He held a rag in his broad, horny hands, wiping his brushes very carefully. He raised his head slowly, like a sheep.

'Don' mind me shoutin', will yer?' he said with ponderous humour, in a loud, cheerful voice.

'No, I don't mind.'

'Only, yer see, it drives a man daft up 'ere; it's so bloody quiet. You can 'ear a pin drop, up 'ere.'

'I bet you can. It's quiet now.'

He had thrust his face forward in a mole-like way to listen and take in what I said. He did this each time I spoke. His face had the blind, shut-away look of the very poor. On the surface he was always in a stupor, with no thought on his forehead.

'Aye,' he pondered.

There was a charged silence.

'You'll think me a bit queer,' he said. 'Only I don' ha'e many visitors.'

'Nor do I,' I said laughing. 'That makes two of us.'

'Aye.'

He carried his bottle and apple to a shelf underneath the wash-stand, and pointed to the chair.

''Ere y'are. Set down, if you like.'

'What about you? Where are you going to sit?' The sound of my own voice jarred on my nerves; it was too sharp and quick.

'That's all right,' he said. 'I got another chair in theer,' and he pointed to the partition. He went and stood at the end

131

window, stooping to look down into the yard. He wore a shapeless blue seaman's jersey. Near him I saw a small iron stove choked with dead cinders. The cylinder was fractured at the base.

'I didn't know if I should find you in,' I said awkwardly.

He was still at the window. I was reluctant to speak, yet I felt myself losing contact with him, a barrier of strangeness building up invisibly between us. He hardly knew me. No doubt he distrusts me, I thought. Once more I was aware of someone waiting for me to declare myself and show my colours, as I had been at Kelvin's. 'Whose side are you on?' the man might have asked. This unspoken question hung in the air, over my head. I wanted to say something positive, to leave no doubt in his mind.

But everything seemed odd and unreal in the dying light, and I could hardly believe any other world than this existed. Such questions belonged to the city, the fume of crowds in the streets. They had no place here. I had left the other world behind, when my feet left the coal-dust on the garage floor. Now there was only this room, growing dark, with its two men, its chair, its stove, its bottle and apple, the piece of painted wood, a wash-stand, the three books.

With a faint shock of understanding, I realized that this was what Meluish had tried to do, by coming up here. Each time he climbed up his ladder he made himself inaccessible, climbing up out of reach. None of the harshness of action was in his paintings, or in his loft. There was only tranquillity. I felt the power and beauty of it taking hold of me. Yet I was afraid of it because I thought it would make me unfit for the world. My instinct was to toughen myself.

He stood there perfectly still against the window, facing me. He was like a piece of sculpture.

I wondered if he had heard me. Then he said, 'Oh ah. You'll always find us here.'

He moved towards the partition energetically, but as if his feet were crippled.

'I'll get out t'other piece o' furniture,' he shouted in the silence. He returned in a matter of seconds, dragging a collapsible wooden chair with a plywood seat, similar in pattern to mine. He seemed to enjoy making a clatter. He gave the trapdoor a violent kick as he passed, and it crashed on the floor, sealing up the hole. Dust rose up. His back crouched as he erected the chair over the trapdoor. Then he sat down deliberately.

'Now then,' he said woodenly, ''ow are yer?'

I laughed again. 'You asked me that once. I'm still about the same.'

He stared at me, then let out a great yell of laughter. 'Well, 'ave I?' he shouted, sitting erect on his wooden chair and staring into space. 'You can see 'ow many visitors I get, can't yer!'

For all his noise, he was as remote and hushed as ever. He sat patiently, waiting for me to speak or to go. I sensed that my company had begun to be a strain on him, because we were strangers. I refused to ask myself if I ought to leave. I liked being with him. It was a strange experience.

Then I noticed his violin, hanging up on a nail which had been driven between two bricks. The bow also hung there.

'Do you still play the fiddle?' I asked him. Since I had been with him I had dropped into the vernacular of my own county. Even so, my question sounded ridiculous. I would have liked to obliterate it, hating its insolence. It was the question of a snooping, curious visitor.

'It wants another string. One's nearly busted,' Meluish said, not answering my question.

To my amazement, he went across and lifted the instrument and bow from the wall. Stooping, he found a piece of clean rag under the wash-stand. He squatted on his heels like a miner, dusting the red wood. I was delighted, sitting in anticipation, watching him. I thought, 'He's given up trying to talk to me. I've given him an opening, a chance to do something else.' Suddenly he looked up with a flash of warmth, gazing at me directly. Then his head dropped again.

The room was almost in darkness. He had the violin under his chin, standing erect where he was. He shrugged his thin shoulders, crouching. Then his right arm jabbed the bow across, in a few savage, jerky movements, as he tried to make his left-hand fingers work. He cursed and stopped. The fingering was at fault. He tried again, advancing a few bars, playing snatches of some virtuoso piece I had heard dozens of times. I couldn't remember its title; it was very fast, and full of brilliant passages. He grinned at me out of a red face, then roared, 'Me fingers are stiff!' He crouched over again, his whole figure grim, and each time he darted the bow across, his features became distorted and his eyes closed. Once he tore on without a break for nearly a minute, his face demonic, his mouth twisting savagely in his beard. It sounded magnificent, making my blood beat up, but Meluish kept gasping out oaths. Finally he failed at some double-stopping. He stood up straight and cursed.

'Me bleeding fingers won't work! Put it back, George – bloody well put it back!' he snarled at himself, and turned back to the wall.

'That was good,' I said in admiration. But he came over to his chair glumly, sagging into it as though in disgrace.

'I used to be good, I tell yer,' he said proudly. He held up his hands, looking at them with contempt. 'I'm done with it now.'

He gazed around in surprise, suddenly noticing how dark it was.

'Now what?' he said, scratching his head. 'I ain't got a light 'ere yet.'

'What do you usually do?'

'Nuthin',' he said slowly, and grinned. 'Go to bed. That's abart all as yer can do, if you ain't got any cash.'

He sat very quiet, his thin, large-boned body strewn in the chair, as if exhausted. As I glanced at him, he pulled himself more upright. I was reluctant to leave him, yet I hardly knew why I stayed. There was an integrity about him that I liked very much. Sitting there, my body seemed to be taking on that stiffness and woodenness he had. It was an effort to speak; I did not want to bother. I stared at his large, heavy shoes in the gathering darkness. They rested on the boards, set a little apart, pointing outwards slightly, anchored by their own weight. They were like little symbols of his character.

'Does Elizabeth come very often?' I found myself asking.

He stirred. 'She 'as two evenings off a week,' he said, and paused. 'We 'ave a bit o' cash then, when she comes,' he added with heavy humour. He rubbed his forehead. 'She's comin' Friday. Aye, that's right. Friday. We'll perhaps go to pictures. ... I dunno, though. Perhaps we will.' Again he rubbed his head. 'We'll do summat, anyhow,' he ended drearily, as though dismissing the whole subject.

He got up and stumbled across the boards to a corner, returning with a small canvas, which he propped against the legs of the easel, facing me.

''Ere's Elizabeth,' he stated, and then grunted with laughter. 'I should 'ave shown yer before it got dark.'

Leaning forward, I could see it was a painting of a rather grim-faced woman of about thirty-five, with fair hair and large unhappy eyes. Her shoulders were clothed in a white blouse. Obviously he had painted the truth, what he had seen, and not spared her.

'She's German,' he said flatly, as he took the painting away.

'Yes, I know. Jack told me.'

'Oh ah.' He was sitting with bent shoulders, his hands clasped, staring into space.

'A queer bloke, Jack,' he mused, in a low voice.

'Yes,' I said. 'I can't quite make him out. Matter of fact, I thought of going to see him to-night.'

I told him this, though the idea had only just occurred to me. And I wanted to give Meluish a chance to get rid of

136

me.

There was a moment of silence. Meluish shuffled his feet.

'I'll come with yer, I think,' he said unexpectedly. 'I don't feel like stayin' 'ere now.'

I descended the ladder, waiting at the bottom, while he balanced on the top rungs to lock up, fastening the trapdoor with a brass padlock.

'Not that there's anything to pinch,' he said, following me into the street.

He stuck his hands in his jacket pockets, hobbling painfully at my side. Under the street lights he looked very shabby. I felt suddenly proud and happy, privileged, as though he paid me a great compliment by allowing me to be with him.

There was a small crowd at the bus stop. Meluish muttered, 'Look at all the canaille,' without a trace of bitterness in his voice. He said it almost in wonder. I glanced at him in surprise, amazed to hear this word from his lips; it sounded so fantastic. He was staring down at the pavement.

'There are millions of them,' I said, to let him know I had understood.

'Bloody swarms and swarms,' he said, and then fell silent.

Chapter 11

AFTER this I saw less of Kelvin for a time. The following Monday I started my new job, clenching myself inside like a fist. After the first day it was no so bad; none of them were, to begin with. Then slowly the days would build up, adding to one another, until I felt a huge accumulated weight of boredom and waste rearing up around me. But this took a long time; and now, after the ordeal of the first day, I was glad to escape from idleness and freedom. A dreariness left me, and I fell easily into the mechanical rhythm again.

I had been there a fortnight when I left my lodgings, and took a bed-sitting room near the Castle. It was dingy, but the surroundings were very pleasant in comparison. There was an avenue of small trees, in new leaf now, the green so vivid that it seemed to vibrate. This quiet, broad road ran its sandy gravel to the foot of the rock, joining the boulevard, and the cliff of sandstone rose sheer above it, very high and impressive, with its bushes and pigeons. The square building which crowned the rock was out of sight from this side.

Stella had not got in touch with me. I reasoned that she had probably thought better of it. It seemed senseless to think of trying to meet her again. Now that I had a few friends I felt less compulsion to go; and I was free now to meet anyone I wished.

The weeks passed, and in July, having a week of freedom, I went home to my mother's. I seemed to have been a long time away, and going home was strange. I did not know what to do with myself there.

Coming back at the end of my holiday to that wretched bed-sitting-room again was a ghastly experience. The room was so bleak and ugly that I could not stay in it. Something drained out of me as I stood there, looking at things exactly as I had left them. I ran out of the house and walked quickly into the city centre, where there was movement and life. Then I got on a bus and rode out to Hyson Terrace to see Kelvin, not caring what had passed between us.

I found his place empty, with curtainless windows; no sign of life anywhere. I peered through the dusty glass into the front room. The paintings had all gone. I could see the rectangles of faded wallpaper, where they had hung.

In desperation I started walking furiously in the direction of Chapel Street. I could not get there fast enough, though it never occurred to me to catch a bus.

I had just turned off the main road into the steep street alongside the brewery when I saw Kelvin shambling downhill on the opposite side. He had spotted me at almost the same moment, and stopped dead, his head cocked to one side, with a sad grin on his face.

'Well, well,' he said in a melancholy voice. He stood on the pavement, one shoulder against the wall, waiting for me to cross over to him.

'I've just been to your place,' I told him. 'What's happened?' I threw out my words joyfully, grateful that he was still around. He was a good sight in that ugly district, though it did not look hellish now. A few minutes before it had been evil and dangerous, filling me with dread.

'I'm homeless,' Kelvin said. 'Let's go back to George's place, shall we? Is that where you were going, to see George? He's not there, he's gone. I'm living there.'

We had started to climb the hill, and I looked at him in bewilderment.

'I don't get,' I said. 'What's happened? Where's George, then? What the devil's going on around here?'

Kelvin shrugged his indifference, but I saw that he was growing more cheerful. He had begun to stride out vigorously, his little eyes kindling and blinking.

'Don't ask me, I'm in the dark. I don't know what's brewing for me.' He spoke angrily, but it was overlaid with pleasure, and he gave a short laugh. 'The thing for me to do is to get hold of those Tarot cards and find out what's going on!'

He plodded forward in a mysterious silence, obviously waiting for me to question him.

'What are you doing up here, anyway?'

'I told you – I'm homeless. Chucked out. That house in Hyson Terrace belonged to both of us, you know – me and Cyril. Though Cyril paid the lion's share. Ever since we've been in there we've never paid a shilling off the mortgage – and the queer thing was, nobody did anything about it. It must have been overlooked all that time – Christ knows how. All we paid was the deposit, when we took over . . . that was sixteen months ago. Then the other week, along came a solicitor's bill for all the arrears, and fourteen days to pay. Ninety-odd quid! So we packed up and cleared; my furniture's up here, in George's studio. And Cyril's moved in with his girl friend.'

'They took the house?'

'Confiscated it, naturally. Poor old Cyril's got the worst of it. Still, we knew it would happen before long. We didn't know when, so we just sat tight and hoped for the best.'

We had arrived at Chapel Street and were crossing the granite cobbles of the yard.

As Kelvin climbed the ladder and unlocked the trapdoor, crouching under it, he said, 'I've been sitting here all day wondering if anybody would turn up. Squatting up here like a saint on a pole, waiting for the bloody world to end!'

I hardly recognized the place now. It was jammed with chairs and a table, a bookcase, and even a radio. Kelvin slumped down in one of his own armchairs.

'How did you manage to get all this up here?' I asked him.

'Easy. Through those doors that open into the street – remember? Then we took the partition down and dragged these things through.' He suddenly roared with laughter. 'It looks like a second-hand shop! When George comes back we shall have to pile it up different to this; on the other side of the partition somewhere. I don't know.'

'Where's he gone?'

'George? Oh, he's gone back to his aunt's in Yorkshire for a holiday. That's his excuse. But he's gone to have some lessons in tempera painting from his teacher, an Austrian refugee named Helman, a cripple. Didn't you know about him? He's a sort of genius, though he can hardly use his hands now – a creeping paralysis he suffers from. But you should see his paintings! He's had a rough time. He's the one who gave George the idea of being an artist, and encouraged him. It was when George was up there once, on leave. This cripple, Helman, befriended him, took him under his wing. And George idolizes him, worships the man. He'll come back here, you see, singing his praises, and he'll have a bundle of work just like Helman's. He can't shake him off, he's too powerful an influence. He calls him "master" – it's the truth! Sometimes he gets me to write letters to him, starting off "Dear Master". Anyway, it's a bloody good job he has gone up there, or I should be out in the park tonight. . . . When he gets back I probably shall be. I can't stay here – he's marrying Elizabeth at the end of this month. I'll probably end up by sleeping on Cyril's work-bench at Bulwell. What a lark!'

He had spat out the last phrase; it sounded a queer mixture of sorrow and impatience and disgust. He looked at me craftily for a moment; then his face assumed its familiar expression of a betrayed and crucified saviour, the mouth clenched and reproachful, the eyes sorrowing. Yet he was uneasy in this role; it was altogether too passive for him. He could not move about while he was hanging mute and suffering on a cross. It did not suit him to be still and resigned; so his face changed again, becoming brash and energetic. Now he was the man who leaps forward to embrace life and accept it. He was ready for anything the postman might push through the door. Let the calamities roll – he grew strong on trouble. He was intent on conveying this impression, and it was more like his natural self.

He was recovering, coming to life rapidly, before my eyes.

He even jumped to his feet, so that he could use his hands and arms and body for making gestures.

'There's something else you don't know!' he cried. 'All sorts of weird and wonderful things have been happening lately, you'd be surprised. And this isn't the end, it's only the beginning – that's what I believe. We haven't been turfed out for nothing; it's for some reason. There's a pattern here somewhere. The point is, I *knew* it was finished, that we were in a backwater there, but I wouldn't move. I refused to act. I seemed paralysed, apathetic. That street was evil, I should never have gone there. You know, I could feel the evil collecting in that street like a sump. I told Cyril and he laughed his head off. But I can see now that I wasn't meant to go there; it was a false turning. . . .

'In the end, though, your destiny catches up with you. It's like a dog you keep trying to shake off and get rid of. You dodge round the corner, down an alley, twice round the gasworks, double-quick time, and you say to yourself, "Now then – try and find me!" Five minutes later he comes trotting across the road towards you, wagging his rudder. So why not accept him to begin with?'

He sat down, banging back in the chair, blinking.

'About a week before we cleared out, the police called round. A copper! I always had an idea they were keeping an eye on the house. And the neighbours on either side, they've had their ears flapping ever since we moved in there. You can imagine what they must have thought. Queer people with beards drifting in and out; artists, Russian spies – and the din we used to kick up in that back room, with the window

143

wide open! So they must have warned the police, lodged a complaint. Isn't it ridiculous? One night, about eight, this copper knocked on the door. What d'you think he asked me? "Is this number sixteen?" he said. And it was on the door, eighteen, as plain as his crash-helmet. "I beg your pardon," he said, and was off. Obviously, he was checking up on us. What a stupid lot! Isn't it too silly for words?'

But I could see that he didn't regard it as stupid. Or if he did, he still felt flattered at the thought of it, for he was basking now in his new glory as a suspected person, probably with his name on the police records.

'They've got black lists,' he told me impressively. 'They know the movements of all kinds of people.'

'Now what?' I said. 'What's your next move?' And I looked at him in admiration, still thankful that I had met him.

I thought suddenly that I was still warming myself at his blaze of egotism. Yet long ago I had known that he wasn't the one. He was really searching himself, in his own ambivalent fashion, searching in all the wrong places. We were all searching. We wanted to get rid of our crippling burdens of egotism, all of us. Kelvin made little blazes of his, and that warmed us. But it wasn't enough. If only we could feel our hearts break with love for a leader! I was looking at him, not taking my eyes from his face. Yes, he could easily have been the one. For it would have to be a nobody, just like him, I thought, with no money and no influence – and in just such a place as this. Someone as naïve and isolated as he was, and ready for anything – just as he was! But someone beautiful, who took beauty to himself, to his face and head and shoulders, when you looked at him and knew him for the one.

'Who knows?' Kelvin said, and gave me an enigmatic look. 'It's not up to me.' His words startled me; then I realized that he had answered my question.

He got to his feet. It was almost dark, and he went behind the partition to search for an oil lamp. Eventually he found one and placed it in the centre of the table to light it.

'George bought it for ninepence at a garden fete,' he said, as I looked at it.

It was mounted on a tall brass pedestal, the tarnished copper vessel for the paraffin swelling out suddenly in the middle. From the base to the rim of the glass chimney it was very high.

The lamp's wick burnt smokily and Kelvin bent down to adjust it.

'The first thing I've got to do,' he said, 'is make a bit of money. Cyril says he could do with some help in the workshop for a few weeks, so I expect I'll do that. He can't pay much, but it's congenial work. Who'd give me a job, anyway, looking like this? It's written all over me, what I am. They know instinctively that I'll only upset their apple-cart. You can't blame 'em. As soon as they see me they start making excuses. It's just as well – I can't stick their bloody jobs …

'Cyril tells me what to do, and I do it – he marks everything in advance and lets me get on with it. He's a good bloke, really. Sympathetic . . . . Then I thought I might join forces with you, if you're agreeable – go halves with the rent for a flat, if we can find one. . . . It's just an idea,' he added casually.

His proposal was unexpected and gave me a shock, though I had often thought of it.

'I'm game, if you are,' I said, watching him closely.

'Well, we won't decide now,' he answered guardedly. 'Let it hang fire. Musn't be too hasty about these things – don't want to go rushing in. Gently, gently, catch a monkey. Ever heard that? The Chinese say that; I like it. In other words, you've got to be wily.'

He smiled as if he had said something very clever.

'When do we start the search?' I asked. I had begun to relish the idea.

'Oh, plenty of time. I don't know if it's a wise move, but we'll soon find out when we're together. Never have liked the idea myself; always preferred to be by myself. We'll see. Probably, with our temperaments, we'll clash in no time, and that'll be the end of it. As things stand at the moment, I can't pick and choose.'

Before we parted I gave him my new address.

We had arranged to meet at my address the following Saturday afternoon. Then we would set off in search of a flat.

I was waiting outside the house for him. He sauntered towards me, gazing around curiously.

'Come up for a few minutes,' I said. 'This time I'll be the one to make the tea.'

Entering my room, he said. 'Oh Christ. This would

146

depress me. All this chocolate-brown woodwork – and that shocking green distemper.'

'It depresses *me*, don't worry,' I said grimly. 'I'm never here any longer than I can help.'

He was staring round at everything, arrogant and disdainful. 'And that bed; not even a divan. Like living permanently in a bedroom. Ugh!'

I ran downstairs to fill my kettle at the tap in the kitchen. There was no one about. When I got back Kelvin was standing at the window peering out.

'What's out here – a dairy?'

'That's right. The front entrance is in Castle Street.'

He grimaced. 'Is this the best you could find?'

'The best at the price, yes. They charge me thirty shillings for it.'

'I know, I know. It's disgusting. . . . Where are you going with the kettle now – downstairs again?'

I had forgotten, coming back into the room with it.

'No, on the landing, outside the door. I share the gas stove out there.'

Again he pulled a face. 'I never did like these places,' he muttered. He perched himself on the bed. 'Sordid. Un-aesthetic.'

He produced a local paper from one of his pockets, together with a street map of Nottingham. Then he scratched his jawbone through the beard, and yawned. Leaning forward, he grabbed the oval gate-leg table, pulling it nearer, so that he could spread out the map.

'See this,' he said, and made a circling movement with his

147

finger over the dense chart of streets. I went over to him.

Roughly in the centre of the sheet a triangle had been drawn.

'What are those pencil lines?' I asked.

His head bobbed up and down as he nodded; he was approving some decision he had made.

'Look,' he said, stabbing at the paper with his finger, 'see this point here? That's where I stayed first, my first lodgings; behind the Arboretum, in Byron Street. See that? Then, when I left there, I went over to Clumber Street for a few months. There's the spot. After that I moved into the house at Hyson Terrace with Cyril. That's this dot, here. I've just connected the points, joined them up, that's all. And I think we ought to look for somewhere inside this triangle. It's only a hunch of course. But you notice how these other abodes of mine are all in the same district? I think it means something.'

I looked at him meekly. 'Doesn't it restrict us a bit?'

'Well, let's have a look at the paper,' he said.

When we had found two or three possible ones, we went out into the grey afternoon. It was about to rain.

The Castle rock loomed over us. It was like a huge boulder that had fallen out of the sky and had not yet been cleared away. I thought that once all life here had revolved around it, for miles around. That was natural. It must have been a vantage point, a great natural landmark, dominating the buildings, steadfast and eternal. To crown it, they had built the castle, though that was gone now. But there was always the great rock. Now it was no longer the centre of life; the city had its new commercial and industrial centres. The rock was a museum-piece. It seemed inevitable that one day they would come and dynamite it, blast it to pieces and drag it out of the way, because it represented the past. We walked in its shadow, under the new foliage of its bushes. Pigeons were preening themselves in their holes, high up.

As we came into the boulevard opposite a factory, Kelvin touched my elbow.

'Just a minute, Lou,' he called, running back.

A big, ruddy-faced man in blue overalls had passed us on a bicycle, then pulled into the kerb about twenty yards away. 'How's Jack!' he shouted genially as Kelvin reached him.

They stood talking for about five minutes. Kelvin had his back to me. Once the man gave a high, braying laugh. He had a greasy haversack on his back; I took him for a railwayman or some sort of factory hand. Kelvin was talking rapidly and laughing in snatches, slapping his thighs. He stepped back and made a hesitating movement, as if to go away. I saw the man draw out a wallet and give something to Kelvin. Then he waved his hand and peddled away. I started to walk on, slowly, hearing Kelvin running up to me.

'How's that for luck!' he shouted as he drew level. He was waving a ten-shilling note in my face. 'Haven't seen old Fred Ryston for years. He's the caretaker at the art school. When I was there he used to get hold of cheap frames for me. He used to spin yarns to me by the hour, down in the basement. Fancy seeing him just at this very moment! I told him the whole story, everything. Told him I was really up against it this time, and didn't know where to turn. He pulled this out and asked me if it was of any help. What d'you make of that? I know he doesn't get much of a wage. Well, I'll be damned – Fred Ryston!'

He bubbled with optimism, chattering gaily as we passed down the Long Row. The streets were covered with a restless throng of shoppers. Kelvin was really confirmed in his faith now, and at the very moment when it seemed as if the bottom had dropped out of everything. He kept drumming this point into me, emphasizing and dramatizing it. Nothing could stop him now; he had won back his enormous will to glory. Once more he was the man who sharpens his teeth on trouble; the greater his misfortunes, the more virulent became his defiance. But now he was joyful as well as beligerant. Hosannas jumped up in his eyes; he held them ready like fists.

He strutted along at my side, darting off to look in shop windows, wings of greasy hair flapping over his ears. As we approached the district he had in mind, he seemed to be gazing up at roofs and top-storey windows, and I asked him what he was doing.

'I'm on the look-out for empty rooms. You see them sometimes, over these shops; old store-rooms they never use, that sort of thing. We might get something like that dirt cheap, and we could rig it up ourselves, with a bit of luck, just as we wanted it. I've got my own furniture remember.'

Eventually we found a flat, in Derby Road. It was in the approved district, the end house of a long, three-storey block that had been converted into flats. In some of them the ground floors were occupied by dentists and solicitors.

The two rooms we had come to see were at the top of the house, and comprised the outer corner of the block, so that there were two windows in each room, one in each outside wall. The house was on high ground, the end windows of these rooms looking down into the city. It was an impressive view. The rooms were square, with plain yellow walls and shabby, ordinary furnishings, all browns and russets.

'Go into the other room, if you like, and talk it over,' said the young man, when we hesitated. He was a tenant himself from the floor below, trying to sub-let his top two rooms to ease his rent. He had just finished staining the living-room floor, standing with the brush in his hand.

I had been standing carefully on the carpet. Then I forgot, and steeped back on a patch of wet stain. I had to tear my foot free and lunge over to the door. 'I'm sorry,' I said.

'That's quite all right, it doesn't matter,' the man cried, and sank down on his knees immediately to obliterate my footprint with his brush. The skin on his fingers and on his beaked nose was tight and shiny. He need not have looked abject, kneeling there, but I thought he did. We left him and went into the bedroom.

'What d'you think?' Kelvin asked me. He had lowered his voice, and seemed strangely hesitant and faltering, now it had come to a decision. He was looking at me almost anxiously.

'Let's take it,' I said without hesitation, to make him decide. We had already looked at four, and I was afraid I should end up at my old address again. 'I like the rooms. There's plenty of light up here, and a good view.'

'Yes, I suppose so.' He was still reluctant. 'It's not bad, though it's not really what I had in mind.'

'We can always change it later, if we don't like it,' I said.

He nodded, not answering, and I took this to mean agreement. I went back to the living-room.

'We'll take it,' I announced to the young man, who was still on his knees. He seemed to have found other patches that needed re-touching. 'Right you are,' he said. 'I shan't keep you a moment.'

I told Kelvin that I shouldn't be able to move in with him for another week; I had to give notice to my present landlady. We had already come to an arrangement about the money. Kelvin was broke, so I had agreed to pay the first two weeks rent.

We stepped into the busy street and made for a café.

'I feel a bit queer,' Kelvin muttered, 'as if we've made a wrong move.' He stopped on the pavement and turned round to look at our new home, surveying it thoroughly. 'Anyway, we've done it now,' he said, and went on.

When I arrived with my suitcase on Friday evening, he had begun to glorify the situation. He had retrieved some of his paintings from Chapel Street and hung them up on the walls. The door was wide open, and he was seated at the table, which was littered with papers.

'*Entrez!*' he shouted. 'Come in, partner. Make yourself at home.' And he grinned craftily, waving an arm in his usual style.

I dumped down my suitcase. It was a good start.

Chapter 12

ONE day I noticed a room which looked vacant, over a shabby music-shop a little further up the hill from us, on the opposite side. Obeying Kelvin's advice, I had been watching for curtainless windows. This looked like a disused store-room, the kind of place we could have for a small rent, and do what we liked with. The idea of such freedom and independence attracted me, and it seemed modest and practical, easy to achieve.

When I told Kelvin, he sounded dubious. His spirits were low that evening. He had been out on a job with Cyril, at some factory, and two girls there had giggled at his appearance.

'I get it all the time, I'm used to it,' he said, shrugging contemptuously. But his face was dark.

Also he was sick of being Cyril's labourer. He had been with him for the past fortnight. He felt useless and wasted; it wasn't his work.

'He doesn't really need anybody now,' he told me. 'He knows I need the money, so he keeps me on. Of course, he likes my company; we talk about every bloody thing: philosophy, women, religion – and he's a real craftsman. Patient. Not like me. I get fed up. You should see him, chiselling at a dovetail, paring at it, then trying it, then a fraction more, then trying it again. He'll do that about thirty times for each joint. I get fascinated and just stand there watching him with my mouth hanging open. . . . But he doesn't need me, and I know it. I know I'm superfluous, and I go nuts hanging around waiting for instructions. . . . I've got to be on the go, that's me. While

I'm there I'm not using any energy, and I'm not creative; that's what kills.'

I brought him back to the idea of this room, but it was unreal to him. He was too occupied with his new problem.

'Go round, if you like,' he muttered. 'Why not?'

He sat slumped in his chair, as he did whenever he felt beaten; all sagging and soft and lifeless, with his chin on his chest. He had given up the fight. And the evening was ruined when he did that, as if the fire of life had gone out forever. He was as concentrated a source of death, then, as he had previously been of life. The carpet went greyish, the walls, the furniture, as if he had turned into a monstrous vacuum-cleaner, sucking in all life and colour and smothering it. I suppose his energy and vital magnetism became somehow reversed on these occasions. He always looked so hopeless and sunk in black despair that I wanted to shout an insult in his face, to relieve my irritation.

Saturday morning came, and I went out for our rations as usual, then walked uphill to the shop I had seen. It was locked, but there was a piece of paper stuck in the window, asking customers to call at the bookshop a few doors below. Apparently the music-shop was always closed, and I began to feel excited, taking this for a good sign. I imagine myself marching in on Kelvin, victorious, with everything settled. Occupied with these day-dreams, I gazed in at the contents of the window a moment, standing in the sun.

It was Saturday, and I was free for two days. Everywhere seemed full of hope, the top of my head warm and tingling, the pavement busy behind my back. I felt vacant and empty, but pleasantly so, as if I had only to wait like this, my feet planted on the pavement, staring at an old euphonium, a dusty sheet of music, a plaster bust of Beethoven, with the sun raying down softly on my head in the morning air, with warmth and air and light around me, the river of people flooding steadily past. I felt relaxed and simple, yet as though my life – my real purposeful life – had not really begun; but there was no need to search. I thought, 'I must be empty, and stand on the pavement in front of a shop, ready to be filled like a vessel when the time was ripe.' It was ridiculous, but it was Saturday, and that encouraged me to be ridiculous. I wasn't alive, I thought, but I was ready to be alive. I was getting ready. It was a queer feeling, as though I could go anywhere and it didn't matter. And that was true, nothing mattered, while at the same time nothing was futile or unimportant. 'I must remember especially the trivial things,' I thought, and the thought curled up lazily inside my head, or wherever it was born, as I stood idly in the sun.

I wandered downhill again until I came to the second-hand bookshop. Inside it was empty, but I could hear a soft murmur of talk coming from a back room, through a partly open door. The thought of another person being there made me nervous, as I had to broach the subject of the room. I decided to buy a cheap book, so that I should be at a slight advantage, and turned to examine the shelves.

I found a copy of *The Return of the Native*, and went over to the inner door. There was silence now, so I pushed the door open a little, peering in. I stared stupidly at what I saw.

A slim, middle-aged man was sitting in a disorderly room, opposite a young girl. I did not have time to look at her. They were seated facing each other, and the man appeared to be holding one of the girl's hands between both his hands, leaning forward attentively. I saw this only for a second, for he leapt to his feet nervously as soon as he saw the girl look, startled, towards me. He advanced rapidly, in a desperate hurry, in two long hops, obviously embarrassed, and I was completely put out. The whole scene had surprised me; it was like something out of a play.

'I'll have this,' I said.

He ducked his head, as if very eager to serve me. His movements were so gentle and considerate, his hands long and narrow and hairless, that I felt ashamed in some way. I felt I had betrayed him, and this obscure feeling humbled me.

'Is there anything else?' he asked, and looked at me for the first time. He had fair thinning hair, hanging long and thick about the ears. His face was small and rather weak, with a tender expression about the mouth. When I noticed his eyes they were soft and indefinite; no strength there, but much kindness and good-nature. I liked him at once. He had glanced almost shyly inside the cover of the book to see the price, and handed it back, smiling. I noticed a delicate metal bracelet looping his left wrist.

As quickly as I could I explained about the room, and why we wanted it. The man stood with his shoulders slightly bent, in a listening position, murmuring, 'Yes, I see, I see.'

I must have mentioned Kelvin by name, for he lifted his

head and asked, 'What did you say your friend's name was?'

'Kelvin.'

'I've heard that name. Strikes a chord, I think. Kelvin . . . Did he ever have anything to do with the local writers' club, d'you know?'

'I'm not sure,' I said smiling, 'but I wouldn't be surprised. He's been in almost everything, as far as I can gather. I've not known him very long.'

'Got a beard, has he? Dark, tallish chap?'

'That's him.' I laughed. 'Looks as if his fame's gone before him.'

The man laughed, very softly, like a girl. His name was Thompson. 'Yes,' he said, 'I think I know your friend. Well, I'm afraid there's not much doing with that room. It's been condemned, the whole building. And the fellow who owns the place has got it full of rubbish. But I'll certainly keep my eyes and ears open, if you'll drop in again. Come in any time; I'm always in there.' He pointed to the back room. 'There's usually somebody in there, dropped in for an informal chat, but don't let that worry you. It's a sort of informal discussion group.'

I wondered if he was trying to explain away the presence of his visitor in the room, but he appeared perfectly natural and at ease now. And I felt a glow of real pleasure because of his friendliness.

'By the way,' he said, as I turned to go, 'if you or your friend want any water-colours framing, I can do them pretty cheap. In any case, I'd like to see some of your work, when you come in again. I might even be able to sell one or two for you. I've been thinking over that idea for a few months now – working in some paintings with the books.'

Going back to the rooms, the magic of Thompson's words kept running through me, especially the use of the word 'work' as applied to my paintings. It sounded so serious and respectful that it went to my head, and I felt an enormous rosy surge of confidence and power. It was absurd, I told myself, because he had seen none of my stuff. But I was unable to reason it away. I went back to wait for Kelvin in this exultant mood, as if I had actually been successful and found a place.

When he came in, and told him the story, he was not impressed. I thought I had failed to get over the picture of Thompson, my impression of him; I tried again, over-stressing his generosity and sympathy and willingness to help. Then, slowly, Kelvin warmed to the man. He sat there dreaming up grandiose schemes for the three of us. I could see them taking shape in his mind, and it alarmed me, so I pointed out that Thompson was far from proposing that we should become his partners. Also, his shop was poor-looking.

'All right,' Kelvin said. He sat back and looked at me thoughtfully. 'What I should do, if I were you, is just wander in again, as this chap suggests. Take a few water-colours, and see what he makes of them. Then, if he's still friendly, invite him up here to have a look at these things of mine.' He gave me a mysterious look, smiling queerly. 'Don't tell him anything about them, though. I want to see his first reaction.'

I had to wait for another Saturday. This time it was raining steadily, falling straight down like a wet curtain in the windless air. I ran across the road and up to the shop, carrying a roll of water-colours. As I thrust them under my jacket for protection, the rain eased off considerably.

I was feeling self-conscious and full of qualms now: I wondered if the man would remember me, and if I had only imagined his friendly attitude.

There was a woman at the shelves, so I hung back, pretending to look around. I decided to wait until she had either been served or had gone out. There was no sound from the back room; its door was partly open, exactly as before.

Suddenly Thompson came in swiftly from the street. It startled me to see that he was a cripple. His left foot was withered, and he wore a slipper on it. The foot twisted inwards and dragged along the floor, but he moved very quickly despite this. He spotted me almost at once.

'Hallo, there!' he cried, and smiled with pleasure. I did not understand why he should seem so glad to see me. But if he was being insincere, I was happily deceived.

'I-I've brought one or two things to show you,' I stammered.

'Good – that's good! Go through, will you? I'll be with you in just a second.' He turned to deal with his customer, bending forward graciously, as though he were dealing in furs instead of books worth only a few shillings.

I was glad for the breathing space; it gave me a chance to get a fresh grip on myself. It was ridiculous, the tension in

159

my very blood, whenever I had to meet someone new. It was a sort of fever that I had always struggled against.

I walked into the room without really looking. There was someone in there, sitting in an old wicker chair, hemmed in by all kinds of debris. It was a man. He sat so still that I hardly noticed him, and when I did he made no attempt to speak. His eyes were half-closed. I was so preoccupied that I did not really begin to pay attention to him for several minutes.

I could hear Thompson's soft voice murmuring something, and the woman asking loudly if he would keep back any novels of Ruby Ayres or Denise Robins that he came across.

I found myself grinning at the stranger, who had the faint hint of a smile on his lips. He dropped his head forward, moving for the first time, and sighed heavily. He was a young man in his early twenties, but looking a good deal older because of his heavy, dark face, with thick lips and eyelids, and because of the great weight of boredom and inertia he seemed to have about his whole figure. As far as I could tell, he was short and thick-set. I had an impression of abundant physical energy rotting away inside him for want of an outlet. His face had a sullen, almost brutal expression, and it was only when he spoke that he betrayed his sensitivity.

'What's he doing?' he muttered now, hardly moving his lips. 'Listening to the story of her life?' And his mouth twisted grotesquely as he jerked round his head to look at me.

'Sounds like it,' I said quickly.

160

I had never seen such a chaotic room as this. I gazed round, fascinated. It was like the lair of someone demented, devoid of system. There was filth and dust everywhere, crazy piles of old books, loose paper, newspapers, picture-frames, old maps. Two oil paintings on the far scabby wall were so dark with varnish and dirt that I was unable to make anything out. It was a tiny place, high and square, and somehow a space had been dug in the centre of everything for the wicker chair and a gleaming new oil stove.

Thompson came in, and opened his mouth to say something; then he stopped himself, comically, and peered round the edge of the door into his shop. I tried not to look at his foot.

He jerked back, smiling apologetically. 'No, she's gone, thank God,' he said, almost whispering. 'I thought I heard somebody moving about.'

'That woman,' the man in the chair said, his voice powerful and sleepy. He had spoken in sarcasm. His head drooped again.

'Oh, by the way,' Thompson said, darting a glance at me, 'this is Jim. He drops in for a chat; he's one of the discussion group I mentioned – aren't you, Jim?' He moved jerkily, sharp and bird-like, a vivid contrast to the other man. 'I don't believe I know your name,' he added, and went over to the door again to peep. He did this every few minutes.

I told them my name.

'How d'you do,' growled the seated man, and raised his head sleepily. His eyelids lifted ponderously, like a reptile's.

'Glad to know you,' I answered with stiff refinement, and

felt slightly foolish. I was still clutching my roll of paintings. An absurd thought came into my head: I wondered if 'that woman' was Thompson's wife. Then I had a surprise, for Thompson said next, 'You'll be able to meet my wife – she ought to be here in a few minutes.'

Jim stirred and stretched one leg.

'You live with Kelvin, don't you?' he asked.

'That's right. Do you know him?'

'Not really, no. I've seen him about a bit. What've you got there – paintings?'

I laughed nervously, nodded, and began to unroll them. This fellow Jim seems friendly enough, I thought.

'Oh yes, good – good,' murmured Thompson at my elbow.

'Don't expect too much,' I said, looking round in vain for somewhere to put them. 'I'm only a self-taught dauber; I don't know any tricks.'

Thompson had cleared the edge of his work-table by simply pushing a pile of rubbish off into space. It made a heap on the floor and he steered it out of the way with his normal foot. 'Here we are,' he cried. And Jim stood up, as if at a signal.

'Keep away from the art schools,' he muttered, and added with special intensity, 'They specialise in failures.'

His remarks sounded so drastic and personal that I looked at him curiously. It made me exaggerate my own prejudice.

'Yes,' I said. 'I know what you mean. They've got formulas for everything – that's why I fight shy of them, I think.'

Thompson had taken charge of the water-colours and

162

was leafing through them hastily, nodding. 'Yes, yes,' he was saying. 'Ah yes. . . . Expressionism . . .' He passed one to Jim, who promptly sat down again to study it. After about a minute he passed it back to the other man without a word of comment. I began to feel foolish and an imposter. I did not feel like an artist. All the seriousness directed at those little rectangles of cartridge paper unnerved me. Their edges were damaged, and the rear unpainted surfaces had become stained and greyish. I wanted to take them back and put them out of sight, to get out of the limelight and be natural again, but Thompson was turning to me in perfect seriousness and saying. 'You're gifted, you know. I think so, oh yes. And the exciting thing is, you're a free agent. That's good, isn't it, Jim? There's no knowing what he might do. I like the freshness of these, don't you? Look at these others – this one, especially. Strong, isn't it?'

Hearing something, he hopped across to the door again, dragging his lame foot. 'Excuse me just a minute,' he smiled at me, with his quick, half-impersonal friendliness, and vanished into the shop.

Jim sat looking at the top water-colour of the pile, letting them all rest on his lap, not touching them with his hands. He could have been falling asleep; his eyes were half-closed and his hands clasped. Then he roused himself, grunted, and handed the bundle to me.

'Thanks very, much,' he said softly, 'I don't have to look any more. No, you're not in any snares.'

He looked at me with interest, his mouth almost sneering – though I discovered later that this was a sort of accidental expression, not connected with what he was saying. Perhaps it was his permanent distaste for things, betraying itself on his swollen lips.

'Queer man, Cliff, isn't he?' he said. He seemed to be thinking aloud, and I did not know if he wanted me to answer.

'Is that his name? I didn't know,' I said stupidly.

He looked at me in silence, almost with insolence.

'He's queer, so he attracts queer people,' he said, as if to himself. 'You want to keep coming here – you'll see some weird ones in this back place. Apart from me, I mean,' he added, chuckling.

Thompson came back. There was a moment of awkward silence. Screwing up courage, I asked him suddenly if he would care to visit us one evening, as Kelvin had suggested. He was enthusiastic.

'Let's see – how about Tuesday?' he asked. 'Would that suit you?'

'Yes, any time,' I said.

I heard a woman's high voice singing out. 'Clifford, are you there, dear?' and Jim got to his feet. Once more it was like a signal he had been waiting for.

'Here's Marjory,' he announced, and made his leering smile at Thompson. 'I'll see you on Saturday as usual, Cliff, I expect.'

'Marjory *will* be offended, just as she's arrived,' smiled his friend. Then the woman had put her head round the door, coyly. She goggled in pretended amazement at us.

'Look at all the men in here!' she crooned.

164

'Come in, don't be shy,' said Jim. 'I'm going, anyway, so there's room for one more.'

'Oh, don't go, Jimmie!' cried the woman. 'Don't leave me!'

'Cheerio, then,' Jim said over his shoulder, picking his way out. 'See you again, maybe.'

I realized too late that his last remark was for me.

'Cheerio,' I said hurriedly, dazed by the coming and going.

The woman came and in and occupied the chair. She was fat-breasted and over-dressed, with an ugly, good-natured hose face and a great split of a mouth. I gazed at her in astonishment, unable to believe that she could possibly be Thompson's wife. Compared to her he was a mere wraith, a wispy, frail creature. I saw now how unworldly he really was, how dreamy and unpractical. He was introducing us, and the woman greeted me with a false eagerness that was characteristic of her, yet in no way an indication of her real nature. Beneath her exhibitionism she was really kind and generous. Because her husband inclined towards the arts, to books and paintings, she affected an enthusiasm for them herself which was loud-mouthed and artificial. He had given her my paintings to examine. She was such a naturally gross and materialistic person that it was fantastic to hear these words of appreciation, these echoes of Thompson coming from the vulgar red gap in her long face, and with such an impossible refined accent. She kept it up with great gusto for a minute or two, then it all fell flat. She had lost interest.

'Well, I really must go, dear,' she repeated, and turned to

me again, her handbag clutched against her stomach.

'Don't forget, Louis, you can come *any* Saturday evening you like. Everybody does; they just stroll in and say, "Hallo, Marjory, hallo, Cliff", and I make another cup of coffee. It's rather nice, isn't it, dear? A sort of open house; we've done it wherever we've been. We did it at Cardiff – oh, those Saturday nights at Cardiff! But I must go, I really must. I always meet someone interesting when I come in here, and then I stay far too long.'

I followed her out, slightly dazed, and we parted on the pavement.

'I'll send Clifford along to you on Tuesday evening,' she promised with huge benevolence, beaming at me. 'He's been talking about you such a lot. Goodbye, goodbye, my dear!'

Just as I got back to the flat I heard Kelvin climbing the stairs. Then he came in, a smear of oil on the side of his nose, carrying a long canvas bag of tools. He dropped the bag by the fireplace with a loud crash, and slammed into a chair.

'What a bleeding life!' he said.

Chapter 13

TUESDAY evening came, and we both thought that Thompson had forgotten, or that something had happened. It was after eight. Kelvin seemed unperturbed, and carried on with what he was doing, painting a Blake-like figure in poster colours.

He sat at the table, his legs crossed, daubing away intently.

'You want to try this body colour,' he said to me. 'It's not so insipid as water-colour, and not messy, like oils. Cheap as well.'

He laid down his brush and leaned back, cocking his head to one side and surveying his work. He smiled absently at me, wiping it off in a second and scowling down at his painting.

'If I touch it any more I'll lose that glow around the head; it'll get muddy,' he said nervously. But suddenly he grabbed a brush, screwed its point into a little heap of cobalt blue and stabbed at the paper again. He gritted his teeth, groaning and twisting up his face.

'That figure of yours will jump off the paper if it sees your face,' I said. 'I'll go back into clay again and wait for the next genesis.'

But Kelvin was too busy to answer. The colour was impure again, and he dropped his brush to snatch up a clean one, muttering that brushes were too small and finicky, and that Goya used sticks and rags, and sometimes his fingers.

'What's that row?' he said, pausing and looking up. 'Is that Mrs. Perrin yelling something?'

I went out of the room and stood on the landing.

'Mr. Paul, a visitor for you!' called the landlady from the hall below.

'Oh yes – come up, please!' I shouted.

A minute or so later Thompson came into view, labouring up the last flight of stairs. My first impulse was to go down and help him, but something obstinate and determined about his efforts prevented me. It was painful to watch him, though he had a stick for support, holding firmly to the bannister with his other hand. He had to pause at each step to drag his lame foot level, and it twisted inwards with an ugly movement of its own, like a perverse thing. I looked calmly at him, smiling, as if everything were perfectly normal. But looking into his eyes, I faltered, because of the grimness I saw there, as he mounted the last few stairs. His face was fixed in a small, subtle smile. He wore a gabardine raincoat, and the hand clutching the stick also held a book.

'It's a long climb,' I said as he reached me.

He nodded, out of breath, holding out his left hand. I was not prepared for this, and brought forward my right hand in the ordinary way, not realizing my mistake until my fingers brushed against his. I was flung into confusion and jerked back my wrong arm too quickly, making the whole greeting taut and self-conscious. The man smiled disarmingly and pretended not to notice. But I was disgusted; my poise and naturalness, which I had so carefully prepared, was all destroyed. Tense with anger I followed him into the room.

I was astonished to find Kelvin still at the table, bending over his painting as if utterly absorbed. He did not look up, and Thompson stood uncertainly, just inside the room, not knowing what to do. 'What is he playing at?' I thought, then realized in a flash that it was Kelvin's way of impressing his visitor. He was acting the part of the artist possessed by his demon. I thought it a stupid trick, and a wave of icy fury swept over me because Thompson was so obviously humiliated by this how of ill-manners. In another second I should have shouted something out, but Kelvin suddenly lifted his head as though greatly surprised. Then he bounded out of his chair, making me forget everything, and delighting Thompson.

'Hallo there! he cried. 'How're you gettin' on, like?'

Everything became natural and open now. Regardless of his tricks and poses, which were always childish and transparent, he had a disengaging frankness about him at these moments, a way of shooting out at once whatever occurred to him. It didn't enter my head to introduce Thompson to him; anything like that would have been ridiculous. And he had taken charge of everything, dragging up a chair, taking the man's raincoat, speaking to me now and then in a direct, unaffected way, and even making himself a listener, eagerly attentive to whatever Thompson had to say. I watched him as he attended to every word of the other man. Though he sat still, perched forward on his chair, I felt that he was really brimming with energy. But he held himself in check, apart from a sudden loud shout occasionally, or a rich, coarse laugh, which made Thompson's eyes open wide and sparkle with appreciation.

'I told Louis, I thought I knew you,' smiled the bookseller, turning his head slightly to glance at me. Really he had eyes only for Kelvin, and I sat to one side, glad to be able to listen and observe.

I was enjoying myself immensely. Kelvin was turning the visit into a success. I felt proud of him because of the seas of life he unleashed in people when he was like this, and I could see that Thompson was affected by him.

'Oh yes, at the writers' club,' Kelvin answered. 'I remember one night there, when some old sod took objection to something I said. He told me I was being offensive. Me!'

Thompson gave a shy laugh, glancing briefly at me again, as if he must communicate his delight, his thin face animated with excitement.

'I can't remember that,' he admitted, chuckling. 'What a shame I missed it. Yes, they're nearly all like that, I'm afraid. I wonder who the "old sod" was – though I can guess.'

He got up to look at the paintings. A few of mine were tacked on the wall above the mantelpiece, looking very pale and weak compared with Kelvin's framed oils. But Thompson limped up to them and stood there respectfully for a moment, leaning on his stick. I studied his face, but could not tell if anything was happening inside him. Probably not, I thought. He murmured some words of appreciation, kindly and irrelevant, while Kelvin restrained himself with difficulty, struggling to be tolerant and perceptive. He had had told me before he could not make head or tail of my stuff. I believed him. He was sincere in his sympathy towards me, if only for the reason that he had been jeered at so much himself. But he appreciated only what was strong and obvious and violent with movement and drama. Stillness was a sign of faltering and weakness to him.

'If you'll let me have a few of these, Louis, I'll frame them for you and put them in the shop window,' Thompson was saying. 'You never know. I thought of putting in some reproductions of moderns, anyway. What d'you think?'

I told him that I was willing, and thanked him. His quick turning aside told me that all this had been a preliminary to his viewing of Kelvin's work. But I did not mind. It was a relief to escape into the background again. Kelvin had wandered over to his biggest oil, as if by accident, and as soon as Thompson spotted it, he exclaimed:

'By God, yes – I like that, Jack! How long ago did you do it?' He rested his stick against the wall and bent down, holding on to the back of an armchair for support. Then he stood up, turning to Kelvin impulsively. 'Wouldn't it make a splash in my shop!'

He went from one painting to the next, carefully examining each one, until he came to one of a female nude, standing at the entrance of a bedroom. Thompson pointed and laughed.

'I see you've put in the pubic hairs. Good for you.'

'Why not?' Kelvin asked in genuine amazement.

Thompson faltered a moment, then grinned. But I noticed a different look creep over his face. I thought, 'I wonder if he expected a different answer, and now he's not certain of his ground?'

Again he pointed with his stick. 'That would go down well with my pornographic clients,' he said looking fixedly at the painting. He laughed softly. 'I could keep it in the back room with a curtain over it, couldn't I.'

I looked at him sharply, thinking he must be joking. Kelvin gave a snort of derisive laughter. 'For the special customers – that the idea?' he said. I knew he was angry.

'Yes.'

There was a little silence. Then Thompson went on blithely. 'I bet the word would spread like wildfire. They'd come flocking in to have a peep at that.' He turned his head towards Kelvin and said abruptly, 'May I sit down a moment?'

As he lowered himself into the chair he began to talk of an idea he had for producing painted horoscopes.

'You know the usual idea – I've done it myself. You get the date of birth, and make a delineation that's based on the zodiacal position of the sun on that day. There isn't much to it, and I've done a fair amount; but my idea was to give them a sort of symbolic picture, based on the delineation. Not too obvious and diagrammatic, of course, but embodying the astrological signs. What d'you think about it? I think it would sell, you know. I've had the idea for some time, but so far I've not managed to find anyone to paint these pictures for me.'

He seemed to be speaking to both of us.

'Jack's your man for that job,' I said. 'He could tackle it; but I couldn't. I'm not virtuoso enough.'

'It would be rather restricted, not a lot of scope for originality,' Thompson went on. For a moment he looked almost ashamed. 'I mean you'd have to use certain colours to suggest the symbolism. But I don't see what's to stop you from working in ideas of your own. If you like, I could give you a delineation I've worked out, and let you see what I mean. See if the thing appeals to you.'

'I don't mind having a go,' Kelvin said. He looked pleased and flattered, but I thought he would soon lose interest in such a scheme. I found it hard to imagine him in any partnership.

He had sat down at the table and was toying with a brush. Thompson let his gaze wander round the room. He told us that it was a great pity, and a mystery to him, that we could not get recognition or encouragement. He had seen so much trash put out by professionals. At this, Kelvin leapt up, his lips writhing back from his teeth.

'Recognition?' he spat out, and put all the bitterness he could into his laughter. 'Recognition? You don't know the half of it?'

Then he acted it all for us, the 'whole story', stabbing the air with his hog's-hair brush. He would have been speechless with his arms strapped to his sides. Yes, he had gone to all the famous names, and as he spoke he ferreted vigorously in a suitcase, pulling out files of letters to show us. He had been on pilgrimages to Matthew Smith, to Augustus John, to Frank Brangwyn. Each time there had been some accident, an evil wind blowing that day. Matthew Smith had been on the verge of influenza, but even so he was sympathetic, asking about Kelvin's other paintings and telling him to come back again.

But the writers had not been so generous, 'a lot of bastards,' in fact. Most of them had snubbed him. Jean Cocteau had written him a friendly letter in French, but he could not raise enough money to pay him a visit, and there was the language difficulty.

It was a powerful performance. I watched him with pride, as if I were putting on a show and he was my star performer. He seemed to have a genius for expressing hatred, for communicating his indignation. As he fed himself with misfortunes, memories of insults, slights, misunderstandings, he was like a big, scrawny rooster, black and wild and tufted, filled with a crooked flame which bent him in all directions, contorting the truth to serve a roosterish pride; and he kept striking and beating the air with his thin, long arms, his voice angry and strident, his little eyes tight with excitement and continually watchful, sparking with a black fire.

He calmed down a little. Going back to his chair, he gave a huge shrug, turning down his mouth in disgust, as if to say, 'It is all of no importance, not worth discussing. Change the subject, talking about something else; the whole thing bores me.' But soon he was off again, this time at a steadier pace, leaning at Thompson in a mild passion of frustration.

'I've had help of one kind and another,' he said. 'People take a liking to me, so it seems – or they hate my guts. Anyway, I've had plenty of hand-outs, tips, sympathy, pats on the back. "Wish I could do more, Jack, but here's a quid" . . . you know the way it goes. I'm never afraid to hold out my hand. Sponge on my own grandmother, if I'd got one . . . why not? My old woman's always giving me money, whenever she's got a bit – she likes to do it. All right, so

I'm a rotten sod! But why doesn't somebody come along and be my patron? Is it my stinking luck, or what? It's happened to other people, so why not me? I've put adverts in the *New Statesman, Times, Spectator, Daily Telegraph*, both the local rags. Old Lou, here, turned up as the result of one. Queer life, isn't it? Yes, I've had plenty of help, plenty – perhaps more than I deserve, when you consider the way I treat people. But it's always on the instalment plan, never enough to get my teeth into. . . .

'What's the answer, Mr. Thompson? What am I doing wrong? How can I get me a sympathizer with a fat backside and deep pockets, d'you think? Have a good look at me, Mr. Thompson! Is it my ugly mug, or what? Tell me how to go about this business, as you're a man of the world, etcetera, etcetera. Just tell me what to do and I'll do it, chop, chop . . . that's the state I'm in at the moment. . . . I dunno!'

He gave a big sad laugh and sat back.

'I dunno,' he said. 'Do you?'

Thompson smiled his amusement. But he was genuinely moved. He seemed to be casting about, trying to think of some practical gesture he could make. Then he said, thoughtfully, in real earnest:

'It's wrong, you know. What a pity! All this talent going to waste. What a pity! Something ought to be done.'

At last he got up to go, then remembered the book he had brought with him.

'Thought you might get a kick out of it, Jack,' he said awkwardly, and tried to force a broad-minded grin on to his face. 'Jim got it from Paris,' he explained, turning to me.

'It's more than just another pornographic book. . . . I haven't read anything quite like it myself. Impressive, I thought. It makes Sartre look like an old maid. Have you read Sartre? Have you read *Intimacy*, or *Iron in the Soul*?'

I had to admit that I hadn't. 'I've heard of them,' I said lamely.

He nodded, not listening. Already he was at the door. I felt that he was preparing some kind of farewell speech in his mind, but he may have been thinking of something else.

'Goodbye,' was all the man said.

He paused a moment with his back to the room, his head half-turned, in a queer listening position. It was as if he stood waiting to be released.

'Cheerio,' said Kelvin, in the curious deflated voice he used for partings. He seemed to hate the thought of being deprived of company, though he would never have admitted it. He sat motionless at the table, looking down at his unfinished painting.

I went down the stairs behind Thompson, to see him to the door. We descended slowly. As I watched his back, set with the same grim determination, I knew I had been right not to offer him assistance before. He rejected help as he would have rejected pity, I thought; in silence, making his back rigid. It was if he had decided long ago that his foot was a mere obstacle to be surmounted, a handicap dragging him back a little; and men could have far worse things than lame feet dragging at them.

It was darker as we left behind the light from the room above, though I had left the door wide open.

'Shall I go down and switch on the hall light?' I asked, when we reached the landing.

He shook his head. 'No, thanks; it's quite all right,' he said politely, and went forward steadily to the edge of the last flight, gripping the bannister.

We were in the street. I stood with him on the pavement, shivering slightly in the cool night wind. I wished I had remembered my jacket.

Now that Kelvin's influence was absent, a formality rose up between us. The older man held out his hand, saying with a smooth kindness:

'Thank you very much, Louis. I've enjoyed myself tonight. No, don't bother. I only have to cross over the road. The bus picks up outside my shop and takes me right to the door of the house. I'll be home in ten minutes.' He smiled, looking into my face. 'Isn't Jack alive! He's a real tonic, isn't he? He really does intoxicate you with his zest and enthusiasm.'

'Yes, he does,' I said proudly.

'I must tell Catherine about you both. She's a friend who comes into my shop quite often. Anything to do with artists and paintings is like a magnet to her. I know she'd love to see those paintings you've got up there. You'll have to meet her. She's a widow, quite young – her husband was killed in the Air Force. If you come round one Saturday evening to our "open house" you'll see her. You're both very welcome. And I must see about your water-colours, about framing them, if you'll let me. I'd like to find a space in the shop for that one of Jack's too – the J.C.'

I was bewildered. 'The – what? Which one is that?'

'You know, the Jesus Christ. His big, fiery one. It's splendid, isn't it? I'm not just being magnanimous – I do honestly think it would attract some custom. But he's a man who should be helped, I think, if it's possible. Do you know the story of Frederick Rolfe – Baron Corvo? Jack's story reminds me a little of his, you know. I've thought of writing a novel based on that theme – but that was years ago. Laziness is my downfall.'

He looked at his wrist-watch. 'Look, I must go. Thank you again, and don't forget what I said!'

I watched his slight figure limping away swiftly, up the hill. On this street the trolley buses were scheduled so that one rumbled below our windows, either up or down, every three minutes. Now it was the quiet interval, with dusk settling heavily into the street. In the unnatural hush there was a faint trembling in the air, a trembling and thudding of far-away traffic. I ran back into the house.

I climbed the stairs quickly, eager to tell Kelvin about our new friend's suggestions, to talk over everything that had happened, and tell him what I knew of the mysterious Catherine.

As I went into the room I was on the point of saying, as a joke, 'The Lord's been good to us,' but something about Kelvin's face stopped me. He had glanced up and was smiling forlornly.

'What's up?' I said.

He gave me a queer look and shrugged. 'Nothing.'

'Don't you like him?' And I thought, 'Damn him and his moods; he's like a woman.'

'Who – Thompson? I like him, of course. He seems a sympathetic bloke, far as I can see. Yes, I like him all right.'

'What's wrong, then?' I demanded.

'Wrong? Nothing's wrong, yobbo. Everything's wonderful!' He laughed ironically, his mouth twisting and hardening as he looked at me.

Deciding to ignore his mood, I told him of Thompson's conversation outside on the pavement. He cheered up at the mention of his picture, beginning to pay more attention.

'Seems a decent enough bloke,' he said. 'Don't you reckon so? Not many as generous as that – though I'm dead wary, Lou. I've had too many let-downs. . . . Wants the Risen Christ for his shop, does he? Queer place for Christ to rise, but that's life! I'm willing anyway. I meant what I said tonight; I'm ready to try any bloody thing.'

'Why not?' In the hurry to cheer him up I had used one of his own expressions. 'Going to have a go at those horoscope paintings?'

He jerked up his head very quickly, and I realized that he had misunderstood me and suspected a challenge, a taunt behind my words.

'I might do – I don't know yet,' he said carefully, his eyes so shifty that I wanted to laugh. Instead I pretended to be envious of him.

'You could make a success of it – not me. You've got more technique, more facility,' I told him. Which was perfectly true.

His face brightened with pleasure.

'No! I'll tell you what makes me uneasy,' he said, confiding

179

in me at last. 'Did you notice how he changed when he got on the subject of pornography, and having that nude of mine in his back room with a curtain over it, for the degenerates to sniff and slobber over?' He was silent for a moment, then he snorted, almost to himself. 'What's he getting at?' And he gave me a shrewd look. 'There's something about him, you know . . . behind his friendliness . . . I can't put my finger on it yet, but I can sense it. Soon as I set eyes on him, I said to myself, "Hallo! now what?" And this pornographic book he's left behind, like a bloody visiting-card – what's his game? What's up with the man – is he impotent, or what? You said he was married, didn't you?'

'I met his wife last Saturday,' I said, and felt important.

Kelvin shook his head, baffled. 'Maybe she's frigid, or playing round with somebody else. Is she an intellectual type?'

'No, she's not like that. She looks like a Jewess. Big, fleshy woman.'

And Kelvin looked at me mournfully. He picked up the book and flicked through the pages, as if seeking an answer there.

'Beats me,' he muttered, letting his head droop forward on his chest. 'What do they want this stuff for when they can get their hands on the real thing? Here's us, itching for a bit of conjugal what-not, and the bird messing about with descriptions of it! . . . And I'll tell you something now: I felt uneasy when I shook hands with the man. Ah yes. Not that there's anything evil in him; no, I don't think that. But he's weak. It's in his face – notice that?'

When he had exhausted this line of thought I told him again about Catherine, wanting him to say something about her. But he refused to speculate. 'If it's in the cards we'll meet the woman,' was all I could get out of him.

'Damn the cards!' I laughed. 'I want to get on with my married life!'

The other man shook his head sadly over my folly.

'Don't force things. Patience, my lad. Learn to wait. Gently, gently, catch a monkey.'

'Who wants a monkey?' I shouted.

For answer Kelvin let his tongue loll out over his lower lip, comic and stupid. Then he rolled back his eyes and leered, like a bawdy clown.

He decided he would have a bath before turning in, and went out on the landing, on his way to the bedroom for his towel. Suddenly he stopped, and I saw him peering over the rail, down into the dark well of the stairs. The bathroom was down there, on the landing below.

He flung back into the room, cursing softly, hooking the door back with his foot so that it shut with a crash.

'Mrs. Perrin's in there again,' he mouthed furiously. 'Every time I go to have a bath, *she's* there. Ah, that's the worst of these places.'

He lashed about the room for a few minutes, jerky and irritable. Half an hour later we were in bed.

Chapter 14

ANOTHER Saturday had come, a warm, cloudy morning. I lay in bed, not properly awake, realizing slowly that I was alone, that Kelvin had gone off to work as usual and that I did not have to go. It was a luxurious feeling. The week-end stretched out before me, free and beautiful. This was the best time, I thought gratefully, when it was all waiting and unused. Then I got out of bed, not wanting to waste any of it. As I dressed, I remembered the unknown woman, Catherine, and Thompson's shop, and the rations I had to buy, in that order.

I went down to the bathroom shakily, with feeble, sleepy legs. I had to steer myself along and hold on to the bannister, as Thompson had done. But although I felt drained of strength, I was exulting with a sense of being alone and perfectly free.

In the living-room I saw the signs of Kelvin's hurried breakfast and departure: the yellow teapot, the used cup and saucer, the remains of a Ryvita biscuit on the plate, the vegetarian margarine. A bottle of fresh milk stood on the table.

I went over to the sideboard and got out a packet of cereals and a dish. I could hear Mrs. Perrin's small daughter screaming hysterically underneath my feet. Then there was a strange silence, as if no one was alive in the house. It went on and on.

A bus glided down the hill, under the window. I caught a glimpse of its red, shining roof, then felt the whole building tremble to its foundations.

Sitting at the table, I began to eat my cereal; I was too impatient to make fresh tea. The movement of the bus had made me restless. As I looked out of the window, the sun suddenly blazed, rolling from nowhere into a blue hole in the clouds. The room was flooded with lovely golden light.

Soon afterwards I stood in a little queue in the low-ceilinged grocer's. I found myself drawing pleasure from this contact with strange people. The girl at the counter furrowed her brow anxiously over each column of figures, obviously flustered, and a man with a grey, waster face kept shouting across bullying questions. He was operating the bacon-slicer, and seemed to be the owner. He darted angry glances at the growing queue, then blustered at the girl again. I began to feel hot and humiliated by the man's boorish behaviour in front of everybody. In the end, though I despised the man, I was irritated myself by the girl's slowness. She wore a little gold crucifix, which swung out from her dress as she bent forward.

At the bookshop I found Thompson in the back room, talking to a man I had not seen before. I hung back, glancing nervously at the shelves, until he noticed me and called me in. Both men were standing, and Thompson smiled and motioned to the chair, making no attempt to introduce me.

'You know that joke, Cliff,' said the other man, going on with what he was saying.

I raised my eyes to his face. It was narrow and white, with black, straight hair and eyes set deeply in the pallor. There was something wrong with this face, I thought. I would not have wanted to touch it.

'No, what's that?' said Thompson. Then he leaned down quickly to me and whispered, 'Shan't be a minute?'

I was too surprised to reply, not expecting anything like that in front of the other man, who seemed oblivious of everything.

'About the lad in the antique shop,' he was droning on. 'His boss said to him, "Just finish putting those worm-holes in that Rembrandt, then you can go to lunch." Haven't you heard that one? It's the stock joke of the trade.'

He stood there stupidly, a thin smile flickering on his mouth. His white hands hung motionless, curled up against the black cloth of his suit. They had broad, flat nails.

'I can't say I have,' laughed Thompson falsely. 'Anyway, Tom, I'll see you in the week, shall I, about those maps you wanted?'

The man was moving off like a phantom, nodding. When he had gone Thompson turned to me, laughing contemptuously. 'Poor old Tom! Bit queer in the head. Been so long in the antique business he's beginning to turn into one!'

I sat bunched in the wicker chair in the midst of the rubbish, not really wanting to speak, gazing around curiously while Thompson sorted through the debris on his work-table. Near his right hand there was a partly-framed picture which had been painted on cardboard. It was a small landscape in the Van Gogh manner, with all the restless and violence exaggerated.

'Who did that one?' I asked.

'What – this? Oh, one of the patients at the hospital; I don't know who. A nurse brought it in to be framed. Not bad, is it?'

I said something, but the painting gave me a strange feeling. I felt dreary, and all the emotion drained out of me. All at once paintings were meaningless; I did not understand their importance. Like a man who has lost his memory, I sat there blankly, struggling to remember the significance of this art. But the creaking of the wicker chair beneath me seemed more meaningful. I struggled to understand the simplicity of my thoughts, wondering if my mind had begun to grow stupid, and I stared hard at the piece of cardboard, trying to respond. It was no good. All I could see was a piece of cardboard covered in oily pigment.

Thompson had moved into the shop, hearing a movement. 'Yes, let me see – that's a shilling,' I heard him say pleasantly, and then he limped back through the doorway.

'I don't think I can change it – just a moment,' he called, hurrying to a box of money and rummaging in it. 'Have you any change, Lou?' he asked as he searched. 'Doesn't matter if you haven't; I'll have to go next door. I want two sixpences, or a shilling.

I looked at his slight figure, which was like that of a boy.

'Here's a shilling,' I said, holding one out.

'Do you mind? I'll have to owe it you.'

'It doesn't matter.'

Before he came back, I got to my feet, and when he saw me standing he looked surprised. I noticed again his fine, pale hair, which he let grow thickly so that strands of it touched his ears, though on the top of his head he was almost bald. And I saw his frail hands. 'The hands of a cripple,' I thought, not quite knowing what I meant.

'Going already?' he cried, too spiritedly. 'Did you bring those water-colours, by the way?'

'No,' I said, 'but I will do. I didn't know how busy you were.'

'Bring them in, bring them in,' he said, smiling and bustling around me. 'It won't take me long to frame them, they're only small. I'll do half a dozen. Besides by having them around I might have someone notice them. You never know. I get a lot of people in here from the University.'

He stood in front of me, looking into my face with a charming eagerness for a moment, his slender body poised lightly in the creased grey suit. Though he was rather an abstraction to me as a man, I felt a pang of gratitude. There was no need for him to be so considerate.

'Shall I run over and get some now?' I asked, and he put a hand on my arm, persuasively.

'No time like the present,' he said.

I went out into the street, blinking in the sunlight, still feeling Thompson's delicate touch on my arm. The pavements were already filling with Saturday shoppers, and the gay colours of the dresses, the glowing faces and soft flesh of the women, sent desire into my limbs. I darted across the road and into the house, which was dark and cool, with a dim greenish light in our top rooms.

I suddenly felt exhausted below the waist, and thought of lying down on the bed. But there was the lure of the busy street, the sunlight on the movement of colours and soft flesh. I gathered the paintings together quickly in a folder, listening for sounds. There was no sound. The house was empty. 'This is why I must get out again,' I thought; 'because all life is in the sun, outside these walls, flowing past in a great swift rush.'

Going back up the hill, something made me start to run. People stared after me curiously, but I ran until I reached the shop. By then I had begun to sweat and feel hot.

I made to go straight into the back room automatically, then stopped myself as my heart gave a little jump. I had heard a woman's voice. Then I saw that the door was almost closed. For a few seconds I was thrown into a panic, wondering what was in store for me; then I took a deep breath and tapped on the door. My instinct, as always, was to go away, to avoid this new meeting. It did not sound like Thompson's wife.

There was a scraping sound, and Thompson's face peered round the door.

'Come in, old man,' he said. All the warmth had gone out of his voice, and he spoke as though he were meeting me for the first time.

A woman sat in the chair I had just left, and the bookseller was introducing us. He did it gently, but he seemed preoccupied and somehow different. I wondered if he was angry with me because he could not be alone with this woman.

It was Catherine, the woman he had spoken of. I wanted to be calm when I looked at her, so I managed to avoid her face.

'Are those the water-colours?' asked Thompson affably, and I gave them to him.

'Aren't you lucky!' he cried jokingly to the woman. 'This is one of the young men I was telling you about – remember? And he's brought some of his work; here you are, dear.' I felt relief racing through me as he handed over the folder. His little speech had made me horribly self-conscious. I stood there blank and stupid, my throat thickening, and I knew better than to try to speak.

As the young woman took the folder and bent forward slightly over it, I was able to look at her. Thompson had moved across and now stood beside her, gazing down. I saw his hand move slightly, rising, then fall back to his side, and I felt sure he would have put his hand on her shoulder if I had not been there.

She had a beautiful white neck and short, springy hair, the curls fair and natural. Her body leaned in the gilded chair, plump and graceful, sitting without affectation, the legs slightly apart, and I had an impression of frankness. When she lifted her head to speak I was amazed to find that my nervousness had almost gone.

'I like some – like this, for instance,' she said in a quick breathless voice. 'But I don't like these Picasso-ish ones.'

'I see,' I said, and laughed. Her face was pale, small and rather strained. She looked at me very seriously and boldly with a modern look which seemed to say, 'Nothing you can tell me can possibly shock me.' Her mouth was set a little grimly because of this nervous, steely boldness. I meant to go on, but fell silent and rubbed my warm hand over my upper lip, staring at my shoes. The room went chilly and awkward, and Thompson had to come to the rescue.

'All the same, there's definitely something original here,' he affirmed. But his voice had gone dull and lacked conviction. I wanted to change the subject, but did not know how to accomplish it. To my astonishment, I found myself staring fixedly and desperately at Catherine, asking her in a strained voice if she would like to come up for tea one day and meet Kelvin.

She looked at me with a smile tinged faintly with triumph, but her eyes were startled. I became conscious of the vulgarity of my suit and white shirt, realizing suddenly how fantastic the suggestion must have been to her. There was a little pause, and I thought she would refuse. Then she glanced flickeringly at Thompson and said she would love to come, asking me to state a time.

Not expecting this quick transference, I blurted out in confusion, 'You can come today if you like.'

She shook her head. 'No, I can't manage today, I'm afraid. Will next Saturday do?'

I nodded dumbly. I felt disgraced because I had not realized that a woman must be allowed this reticence, this graceful strategy, but in the midst of my shame I thought of how cool she looked in the blue-grey dress.

There was another painful silence, and Thompson broke it by scuttling into the shop to see a customer. I seized my chance and started to walk out after muttering 'Goodbye.'

The woman still had my paintings on her lap, pretending to look at them. She called after me, 'You've forgotten these!'

I turned round jerkily, saying that Mr. Thompson was going to keep them for me, and she blushed and nodded, laughing childishly. 'See you next week, then!' she cried in her soft voice, which inclined to huskiness.

I went back to the flat. I began pacing up and down, trying to absorb my impressions and regain control of myself. Long before Kelvin came I was itching to tell him about this meeting, though I guessed he would feign indifference. By now I knew all his different reactions to my bits of information. If he did not pretend to be bored, then he would brood, or scoff, or else launch into a sermon. He was perverse, temperamental as a woman, and usually he liked to be as annoying as he could, for the fun of it.

He was late this Saturday. It was early afternoon, and I was at the window, looking down into the street, when a motor-cycle drew in to the kerb a little further down, and Kelvin got down from the pillion. I guessed that the other man was Cyril Cooke, the joiner, the man I had not met. He was wearing a dark leather helmet, and large celluloid goggles obscured his face. I saw him drive off, giving a brief wave, and Kelvin came towards the house.

He stumped heavily up the stairs and came in, banging against the door. My heart sank when I saw his face; it was set in long lines, with that sullen, self-pitying expression.

''Allo,' he said, twisting his face. And for an instant I was intensely sorry for him. He seemed so childish and subjective, so at the mercy of the world. He had surprised me when he spoke, for a small, gentle voice had come out of him.

I told him cautiously that I had invited Catherine.

'Well,' he sighed, weary and condescending. 'I only hope you know what you're doing.'

He was rummaging around in the cupboard, gathering together his dirty laundry to send off to his mother.

'Why?' I asked. Suddenly I wanted to provoke him, to turn the tables. I had been listener long enough, I thought, beginning to bristle up. It was something I did periodically to maintain my self-respect.

'Why what?' He peered up at me, deliberately stupid, cramming soiled underwear into a linen bag.

'What harm is there in that?' I demanded.

He pushed in the last shirt and began to fasten the mouth of the bag, suddenly very busy. He sighed massively.

'She's a widow, isn't she, this woman?'

'I think so.'

'What's her name – Mrs. . . . what?'

'Thompson didn't tell me.'

He shook his head. 'No good,' he muttered gloomily.

'Why not?'

'You can't break up things like that, even though the bloke's dead. He's there all the time, like a ghost. Very often more powerful than when he was alive. Women always hark back to the past. They feed on memories, women. If there was anything between them, it'll be there now. No. Not me. I don't want to get mixed up in it.'

'How d'you know what the situation is,' I asked in amazement, 'until you've met her? How d'you know there

191

was anything between them? She didn't strike me as being attached to anybody, living or dead. What are you afraid of?'

He glared at me. 'Listen, I'm only telling you what I think. I don't know – how should I? Don't listen to me, do what you like. I tell you I've had a bellyful, that's all. Married women, widows, girls engaged to be married, they're all one to me. I just don't want to get mixed up in it.'

It was a meaningless argument, but I intended to go on with it. The real argument lay under the surface. And his rasping voice, hard and ugly, made me want to fight.

'Don't you believe in fate?' I goaded bitterly.

He went red, and his movements became erratic. But her held himself in check.

'All right, all right,' he said in a low voice. 'You do what you think best. Don't listen to my advice.'

'That's just it, you don't advise, you squash any idea that isn't yours,' I burst out irrationally, regretting my words at once.

He went on with what he was doing, and refused to speak. A few minutes later he was searching for his pen to address the parcel he had ready. He cursed.

'Here you are, Jack,' I said holding out mine. I wanted to restore the naturalness between us, to kill the tension.

'Thanks,' he said shortly.

He used it and handed it back.

'Good old mother,' he said, thumping the bundle with his fist. 'These mothers . . . I dunno . . .' Without explanation he took up a letter lying open on the table and began to read

192

it aloud. 'My Dear Son, I hope you are keeping well and in good spirits. Your father is fine, and I am quite well, only tired sometimes. We often think of you and wish you success in your career as an artist. I believe in you, Jack, whatever it is you are set on doing, even if I do not understand. Here is a pound. With all our love.' He lifted his head, grinning cheerfully.

'Isn't that marvellous!' he bellowed. 'You'll have to go a long way to beat a simple faith like that. And she *doesn't understand*; that's the part that gets me!'

He was almost himself again, boisterous and animal, banging against the furniture with sheer excess of energy. I noticed for the first time how the top part of his body was hulked, insensitive, with the broad shoulders and short neck, and it startled me to see his delicate treading feet, so small and hovering. Instead of lumbering about, which you expected from such a big man, he skipped and pranced. When he exploded it was with his arms and head and shoulders, powerfully, yet his spindly legs and little feet always robbed him of impressiveness. He was too earthy and clownish to be an angel with a flaming sword, and to be like an Old Testament prophet he needed heavy legs and broad feet. He never looked planted on the earth.

Chapter 15

WE left the house together, and descended the long, shop-lined hill of Derby Road. Kelvin swung his bundle from his wrist like a sailor, walking vigorously at my side. His eyes were everywhere, his feet neatly side-stepping as he swayed his body through the pavement crowds.

I saw that the silky air and the sunlight were working wonders on him. He wore newly-pressed olive-green trousers and a neat black blazer with metal buttons, a red-and-white polka-dot scarf carefully knotted and arranged in the neck of his pink shirt. His greased hair kept falling in black wings around his ears, and at the back it touched his collar.

'Be gay,' he always told me. 'Wear bright colours; it's good for the morale.' Acquaintances he met in the street were always amazed at his prosperous appearance, knowing he had no regular job, and suspected him of all kinds of shady contacts. Each time this happened he was delighted. Once, when I was with him, and he caught up with me afterwards, he yelled above the roar of traffic, 'I've got him mystified, he can't make it out! Why should I look like a hobo just because I happen to be a starving artist? What's romantic about that? . . . See this jacket? I've had it six years. I've given clothes to George, you know – all sorts of stuff. He still looks like a tramp. Keith was the same till I took him in hand. No idea. It's a matter of aesthetic with me. And no woman is going to look at you if your arse is hanging out. Know that? Those things go deep with a woman.'

Now he trod the warm pavement and snuffed the perfume in the air, spruce and slick, his gaze fastening on everything female. He bragged to me eagerly of all the things he wanted to do and could easily accomplish if he only put his mind to them. All he wanted was a little help from providence, a breath of favourable wind. He kept brimming over with hope and faith. 'Keep your bowels open and trust in the Lord.'

He dodged into the first post-office with his bundle and I waited on the corner. Joining me again, he hinted vaguely at an appointment he had with someone at the The Nine Days' Wonder, an ancient, smoke-filled tavern built into the castle wall at the base of the Rock. He made his hint so obvious that I said to him:

'Why don't you say you want me to clear off?'

He bellowed with laughter. 'It doesn't bother me one way or the other,' he said, 'Ever been to The Nine Days?'

'No,' I said. 'I've heard it's pretty notorious, of course.'

He nodded. 'Bit of a dive, so they say. Prostitutes hang round there in droves when it gets dark. I like the place myself; it's got atmosphere. We'll pay it a visit one day,' he added, grinning craftily.

'See you later, then,' I said and moved away, releasing him.

He slipped through the crowds like a fish and disappeared. Not knowing what to do with myself, I wandered aimlessly into a cinema.

It was nearing eight when I left, and I turned back towards the flat. The night was falling, yet from thirty yards away I could see no signs of life through the top windows, no

195

electricity burning, no one moving about. The thought of the empty rooms and shabby rented furniture filled me with revulsion, and my feet dragged. I could not force myself in, though it seemed pointless and cowardly, and I hung about in the street for a while, trying to decide my direction. As I thought, I walked slowly away from the city centre, as if I had already resolved to go that way. No ideas came, and my mind began to seize at names. George Meluish, Keith, Stella. I stood at a bus stop.

Finally I got on the first bus that came, intending to go to the terminus and walk out to the open country. Then I discovered that the bus was taking me towards Thompson's district. I had remembered that it was Saturday night, his 'open-house' night, and asked for his road. Sitting in the softly rocking bus as it snored up the unfamiliar hills, the ice in me started to melt. I was thinking resolutely of his rosy invitation. And I desired company too much to be nervous of the strangers, whoever they were. Thompson himself was a friendly enough person, and so was his wife, I told myself.

The conductor called out with bleak efficiency and I jumped off. I found myself in a drab, broad street of fairly large houses, each one with its own hedge or wall boxing in the pocket-handkerchief garden. The evening had turned cold, and I buttoned my jacket as I walked.

Finding the number I wanted, I pushed open the gate, immediately bewildered to find no front door. The entrance was at the side of the house. As I stepped on the tarred path I felt that I was being spied on through the front window curtains. There were chinks of golden light, and sounds of conversation.

I think I had expected to find the door open, but it was shut tight. Before my courage had seeped away I had hammered loudly on the faded brown paint. A tiny strip of paint flaked off and fluttered down at my feet. I heard Clifford Thompson's muffled voice calling something; it sounded unnaturally high.

The door opened. It was his wife. She looked uglier than ever without her coat, with bare arms and shoulders and a great thrusting green bosom. There was something indecent about such an exposure. She stared blankly, her face rigid, not recognizing me for a moment.

'You're not . . .' she began. Then her face creased artificially in an expression of welcome, though the gusto she put into it made the whole act comic and acceptable. Quite unintentionally she made a mockery of formalities. Nothing existed but that tremendous horse-smile, those huge teeth and merry eyes.

I began to apologize for coming unexpectedly.

'Oh, my dear boy, one more won't make any difference,' she cried, taking my arm and steering me down a short passage towards the room at the front of the house.

There were no introductions. Marjory found me a chair and promptly disappeared. I looked around for her helplessly.

Thompson, catching sight of me from the other side of the room, called out, 'Hallo, Louis – glad to see you,' and took no further notice, continuing his conversation. He was talking rapidly to a heavy man in his late thirties, a Viennese, as I discovered afterwards. I thought he was Czech or Polish. I settled back in the depths of my armchair, making myself as small and unnoticeable as possible because I wanted to listen and absorb everything.

I gazed in fascination at the foreigner's swarthy face, his brush of glossy hair, and the large flabby mouth, which had shapeless, rubbery lips. When he laughed, showy and theatrical, the smallness of his neat white teeth amazed me, in a mouth which seemed far too big. His teeth were lost in that cavern.

There was another man, older, a sub-editor of one of the local papers, absorbed in some apparatus in a corner of the room. He stooped over it in silence, dressed in a grey suit.

Marjory Thompson startled me, leaning down from behind my chair to hiss excitedly: 'You've come just right! We're going to have a film show – that's what Robert's messing with over there. Robert, how long will you be? He's brought his cinematograph, but he won't tell us what we're going to see. I hope it's something unusual, something thrilling!'

The man straightened his back, standing a little awkwardly in his loose grey clothes, long and bony, with boyish, curly hair and a quiet, dreamy face. Watching him afterwards, I tried in vain to imagine him in his occupation. Now he made a queer movement of the head and did something grotesque with his eyes, showing the whites, like a terrified animal. It was like a fit, and I dropped my head in embarrassment, ashamed to see him. But no one else seemed to notice. It was a mannerism he kept repeating, and they had apparently grown used to it.

'I've brought *The Cabinet of Dr. Caligari*,' he announced, frowning and smiling. He ducked his head out of sight again.

'Ah,' cried Thompson, who had heard, 'that should be good.'

'Oh yes, simply lovely!' neighed his wife, turning to me with her radiant face and huge, engulfing smile. Before she dodged away to make coffee I caught sight of her shred, twinkling eyes, and decided that she must surely have Jewish blood. There was that mixture of ugliness, the dark heaviness of her flesh, and the almost suffocating welcome, the damp warmth she turned on you. The shrewd, sharp eyes, together with moments of extraordinary sweetness and charm, throwing you off balance. I felt glowing and rosy and quite happy, in an aimless, inconsequential kind of way, after she spoke to me. Her voice brushed against me physically and did this, like something fertile and supple, stirring my blood.

It was a small, high room, with two or three bulky, shabby chairs, colourless, and a rich blue-and-red Persian carpet. The walls were lemon yellow, with Chinese prints arranged tastefully above the fireplace.

I watched everything out of a cold and accurate eye, my warm blood circulating thickly. I was not involved or touched by any of it. Yet I did not feel out of place so much as absent, like a spy, looking in from outside.

The foreigner laughed his sniggering, wet-mouthed laugh

again. Thompson addressed him as Kurz.

'What's the matter with our way of singing, then?' he asked now, smiling and gazing about restlessly. He was in shirt sleeves and cardigan and slippers, looking very much the host. His empty pipe made a moist crackling noise when he sucked at it. He folded his arms, watching the other man's face with amusement and a complete lack of interest, as if the question had not come from his own mouth at all. When Kurz answered, he did not appear to be listening, and had turned his head to look at me, smiling.

'What is the matter, do you say to me?' the foreigner was saying in a thick, loud voice. He was an amateur tenor, and so an authority. 'I tell you it is the matter with all your country, that is what I say, Clifford. Clif-ford, yes, that is what I am saying! A . . . a lack of something . . . from here . . . a terrible lack.' He pressed both fists to the region of his heart and spread his legs, flinging back his large bushy head. It was a ridiculous pose, and I marvelled at his vulgarity. In my first impression, prejudiced by his nationality, I had thought he was subtle.

Thompson had backed away, nodding and murmuring agreement, as if to get out of close range. He sat down, his lame foot thrust out stiffly. 'Ah yes,' he cried, twitching about to get settled, adjusting the cushion behind him.

Kurz flung out his arms dramatically, opening his hands like fat flowers, and as I watched I saw his face grow heavy and voluptuous, his fleshy throat swelling. He sang something rich and turgid out of Wagner, drowning the small room in sound. Then he stopped abruptly, his face aflame.

'It is not just the voice, not only that, Clif-ford!' he panted. 'You have to give it another thing . . . a feeling of . . . yourself . . . how can I say it? It is not to sing enough – no, my English is not good. It is not enough to sing! There! Good! You hear me, Marjory?' he shouted through the door triumphantly. 'Do you agree with what I say, Mar-jory, eh?'

'I can't hear what you're talking about, but the singing was simply gorgeous!' came her voice in a high shriek from the kitchen. 'Do carry on, Kurz! Are you there, Clifford? Ask him to go on, dear, will you?'

The man swung round on Thompson like a bull, his round stomach protruding aggressively. 'What is that?' he asked. 'She wants me to sing more, your wife?'

We were saved by the film.

'I'm ready now,' said Robert shyly. He had come forward unnoticed, and stood with a rolled sheet which was to serve as the screen.

'Can someone help me with this?' he asked, a faint Scottish accent in his speech.

Kurz snapped shut his fatty lips like a fish and squinted round at everybody. He was like a lamp that had been abruptly switched out of circuit, the circuit of the room suddenly by-passing him. It was quite accidental, this ejection. I had seen it happen before. It was cold and odd and very English, but the man stood like a fool, not understanding. It was of no importance, but he was not to know. All at once he found himself ignored, though it was only temporary. He would be switched into the current again in a moment. But now he looked mortified. Without the limelight he was bereft of

201

humour and personality. His face had gone dark and surly, and he wandered over to the piano, arrogant, swaggering his hips, and fingered some sheets of music.

Thompson struggled with his friend to attach the sheet to the curtain rail. They had just finished when there was a commotion at the side door. I heard Cathrine's voice, and then Marjory bustled her into the room. Something jerked in my chest.

'Isn't this nice – both of them!' she gushed. She began to clear books and newspapers out of the armchair next to me.

'What's that?' said Thompson, turning and coming forward. 'Hallo, my dear,' he said to the young woman, lowering his voice and smiling with subtle sweetness. 'Yes, sit down here. How nice to see you. What did you mean, Marjory – how can Catherine be both of them?'

'Oh, aren't you a funny man!' Mrs. Thompson chanted. 'Jim's here, of course.'

And Jim strolled in, adjusting his tie. He made an effort with his face, trying to smile benignly at us, then gave it up.

'Hallo, what's this?' he grunted, and jerked his head at the improvised screen.

'A film; we're going to have a show – *The Cabinet of Caligari*!' said Marjory impressively. 'Did you think we meant a real cabinet?' she asked me suddenly, and gave me a roguish look.

Not realizing that she was joking, I said in great haste, 'Oh no, I've heard of it. Isn't it an old German film, an experimental thing?' I knew perfectly well what it was, but I did not want to sound pompous. Everybody was silent and looked at me; it was the first time I had spoken.

'Expressionism,' Jim muttered indifferently. The whole business seemed to have wearied him before it had even begun. 'Queer stuff, cubistic sets. It's a film classic now.' He broke off and let his head hang, hands stuck in his trouser pockets. He stood there, his stocky figure quite motionless, as if he had gone to sleep on his feet.

Catherine spoke up from the depths of her armchair, beside him. 'When does it start she asked?'

It was a slow, grave voice. I wanted to look at her, but I was afraid.

'Now,' answered Thompson, and gave a sharp smile. He was a different man in his own home. 'We're only waiting for Jim to sit down.'

Everybody laughed, and Marjory came in, closing the door.

'The food and drink is all prepared,' she said contentedly.

I wanted to say something to the woman at my side, to establish contact with her. It was impossible in that crowded room. I stared grimly at the blank screen until she turned her head to speak to me.

'Where's your friend tonight?' she asked, her eyes wide open, slightly astonished-looking. She moistened her lips with the tip of her tongue.

'I don't know, to tell you the truth,' I said, speaking too eagerly. 'He went to meet someone at The Nine Days'

Wonder.'

'Yes, yes, I know,' put in Kurz from the piano, beaming at us. 'It is a strange name for a drinking place!'

There was a general laugh, mainly at the phrase 'drinking place', and the Viennese luxuriated in it like a cat, delighted to be back in circuit again.

'Is everybody ready?' asked Robert, stepping into the middle of the room. He looked so timid and dreamy that I wanted to laugh. He flung back his head, flickering his eyeballs as he had done before, and this time I stared at him curiously, without shame. Waiting for a reply, he closed his eyes and put his head onto one side like a bird. It gave his face a blind look. 'Is everybody ready?' he repeated timidly.

Then Marjory noticed him. 'Oh good, good old Robert!' she said, and told us all to sit still and be quiet. She got up and switched off the light.

The machine whirred a dazzling beam across the room, slanting over my head, the film stuttering into life, hazy and blurred. There was a curtain made up of beads of water, then big velvety smudges of smoke, until the focus had been adjusted.

Marjory had brought in two chairs from another room.

'Isn't it romantic!' I heard her gurgling in the darkness. 'Hold my hand, Jim – Clifford's over there. No holding hands, you two,' she called in my direction.

The picture was steadying itself, sharpening into the entrance of a large, sinister building. I watched the baroque columns growing clearer, streaked with fine lines.

'Look, it's raining!' whooped Marjory. 'Will it be like

that all through?'

'Those early silents were like that,' stated Robert from the rear, in a flat, informative tone, like an official guide.

'Shut up, Marjory,' said Thompson. 'What do you want, Twentieth-Century Fox?'

Then Kurz chimed in, 'Is this German, you say, this film?'

'Yes, early German,' Robert said.

'Aren't the sets funny – all drunken!' cried Marjory. 'It's extremely clever though, isn't it? Especially when you think how old it is. Quite ingenious, really. Oh, what's happening now?' she burst out spontaneously, forgetting to be critical and admiring. 'Oh Lord! look at his face; it's been dipped in the flour-bag!'

In the semi-darkness I managed to look several times at Catherine. She was smoking a cigarette, and, perhaps aware that I was looking at her, he face had taken on a haughty, secret expression. Her features, clear and compact, struck me as being taut and unhappy, her mouth ready to turn down and become a grimace. Now she stared gravely at the screen, and I suspected her of assuming a profile she knew to be arresting. But perhaps it was not pretence, I thought – perhaps it was the influence of the room. I turned back to watch the film, wishing it would end, weary of it, sitting with an icy heart. It was fantastic and unreal, a morbid, sickly thing, full of corpses and somnambulists and petrified anguish. I thought that it should be dug into the earth, to rot away with other things of its kind.

It finished at last.

'What did you think of it?' asked Catherine, her eyes laughing.

'I don't know,' I said.

I wanted to speak frankly, but instead, for the benefit of Robert behind me, I said evasively, 'I've seen it before, a long time ago. Did *you* like it?'

'Yes and no,' she said. 'I can't honestly say I was moved by it, though it must have been very advanced when it first came out. It's cleverly done. Imaginative, in a depressing wa.'

'What's the good of imagination, though, if it makes you feel miserable?' I asked, half-jokingly.

Catherine laughed ruefully. 'Most of the things I like are miserable,' she confessed. 'Why's that, do you think?'

Before I could answer, Marjory had arrived with a tea-waggon; coffee and shortbreads, and a heap of tiny sandwiches.

'Catherine, here you are, dear. I heard what you said, and it isn't true. You like me, don't you, and I'm not miserable! What will you have to eat?'

She ministered to all of us with obvious enjoyment, motherly and affectionate, pleased with her large family.

I found myself looking at the swaying flesh of her shoulders and arms, as she exerted herself. She chatted on rapidly, and the supper became gay and frivolous.

'What's that?' said Thompson suddenly, his coffee halfway to his mouth. 'Listen, keep quiet a minute.'

In the tense silence we heard a scuffling sort of tap at the window.

'Who the devil's that?' said Thompson, staring at his wife.

Then there was a tremendous hammering at the side door.

'I'll go dear,' said Marjory, rushing out of the room.

We all stared blankly at each other, listening. No one had anything to say. We were waiting for Marjory's voice.

'You silly fool, Paddy, frightening us like that,' we heard her exclaim. 'You know very well you only have to walk in.'

She went on scolding the newcomer as he hung up his coat in the passage. Thompson and Jim exchanged significant glances.

She made a triumphant entrance with her latest guest, a young fellow in his early twenties, his soft face unshaven, bleary-eyed, dragging his feet and blinking in the strong light.

'Don't ask him where he's come from,' she sang out ironically. 'It's throwing-out time, and he's tight, by the look of him. Make him sit down before he falls down, somebody, while I get him a cup of coffee.'

Paddy lurched where he stood, but Jim had already placed a chair behind him. He looked around and saw it, blinking his eyes gently, and let himself fall like a sack. It shook a groan out of him, despite his smile. The knot of his tie had worked up under his collar.

'I'm the strongest man in the room, no matter what state of intoxication,' he bragged rubbing his eyes. 'Christ alive, I'm blinded. Clifford, my friend, my stalwart friend!'

Thompson smiled across. 'Hallo, Paddy. Pity you're late;

you've just missed a film. Robert's just shown us *The Cabinet of Caligari*.'

'Intellectual stuff . . . highbrow . . . prefer Guinness . . . Catherine, I love you!'

He peered at us all in turn, then surveyed the room, leaning dangerously from his chair. But I baffled him.

His gaze swung back to me, and he frowned. 'What face is this? . . . Ah, Kurz, my fat friend!'

The foreigner smiled contemptuously, his eyes glinting.

'Drink this and behave, or out you go,' said Marjory, brisk and efficient, coming in with the steaming coffee.

The young Irishman took the cup with both hands. 'Marjory,' he declaimed, 'my bootiful saviour.' He took a sip at the drink. 'Ugh! I'm scalded.'

Then he felt really sick, his face grey, and Marjory took the cup from him and watched in silence, as he hung down from his chair.

'Are you ill?' she asked in compassion.

He made a miraculous recovery, sitting upright, suddenly defiant.

'I want to hear music and poetry. . . . My soul . . . my soul is withering . . . crying for music . . . poetry,' he shouted, out of a white, sardonic face. 'What a snivelling lot ye are, feeding your faces. . . . Music! Poetry!' He hung sideways, towards Catherine, his blurred face lecherous and yearning. 'Or if you like I'll tell you a dirty limerick.'

'Yes, go on,' challenged Catherine, the bold, modern woman.

'You'll do nothing of the sort, Paddy my lad,' giggled

208

Marjory. 'Robert's got a record of John Gielgud he'll play for you, if you sit quiet – the one you heard last time.'

'The Shelley – I'd forgotten that,' said her husband. 'Put it on will you, Robert – d'you mind?'

Paddy sat murmuring, slumped in his chair, sunk back into a stupor again, and Robert went over obediently to the gramophone.

'Which side would you like?' He asked, crouching down, his mouth muffled against his shoulder. No one answered, so he asked again in his soft voice. 'Any particular side?'

'I don't think so, Robert,' said Thompson. 'Paddy won't notice much difference.'

'Yes, put on the exciting side, darling!' ordered Marjory. 'The one where gets passionate and exalted – you know. I could listen to that all night long, it's so beautiful!' She had crammed so much false ecstasy into her voice that I found myself grinning and looking at Catherine, and she did something with her eyes to show that she was amused. I was so pleased by this little triumph of communication that I immediately forgot my tired knees and singing head. I felt proud of the intimacy I had created.

Kurz got up to go. 'I have to do some decorating work tomorrow,' he announced, 'and it is an early time. Now I must go to sleep, if you will excuse me.'

He walked to the door importantly, made a stiff bow, then laughed, as if he had done something very funny. Marjory ran after him to see him out.

She came back when the record was being played, and made a great business of tip-toeing to her seat, her face respectful. The voice droned on, professionally poetic, rising slowly to its timed climax. 'I bleed! I bl-e-e-d!' groaned the agonizing actor, and Marjory gasped with pleasure:

'What a gorgeous voice! Isn't he sublime!'

At this Paddy sat up stiffly, almost recovered. Once more he was the belligerent, wronged Irishman.

'Sure, and if he was living in this day you'd pillory the man,' he spat out in derision.

'Who, Shelley?' said Jim, lifting his head.

'Oh, Paddy, no, we wouldn't,' protested Marjory in a hurt voice. But she was probably finding it hard to imagine such as man alive today.

There was a stir of interest now.

'Have the Irish a better record than us in their treatment of poets, I wonder?' mused Roberts, asking no one in particular.

'Ah, shut your filthy mouths,' broke in the young man brutally. He belched and groaned, closing his eyes.

Marjory shrugged, shaking her head of oily hair.

'I think I'll go, too,' said Jim, rising to his feet wearily. 'It's getting late, and the conversation's too much for me. Anybody else coming? You coming, Cath?' he asked casually.

I held my breath, almost smiling when she shook her head.

'Not yet,' she said calmly, and looked up into his face.

'Suit yourself,' he said. His indifference seemed genuine, and I was puzzled, wondering about their relationship. He stretched himself, yawning, and waved sarcastically at the room. 'So long, folks,' he said, out of his malevolent grin, and went out.

Now there was a lull. I sat on, grimly fighting back my exhaustion. I was not accustomed to late hours.

Robert had stooped down beside Catherine and was saying something about *The Egoist* in his gentle, withdrawn voice.

'Have you read any of Meredith's books?' I heard him murmur. 'He's rather difficult, but well worth the trouble. Would you like to borrow *The Egotist*? It's his best, I think.'

Paddy roused himself. He rolled about on his chair, holding his beard and cursing bitterly. As he slowly revived he became more tragic. He struggled to his feet and walked very carefully until he reached me.

'Don't mind if I talk to you, do you?' he mumbled, sitting down on a stool in front of my legs.

I shook my head, catching sight of Thompson's smile of amusement. The young man had twisted his head round to look into my face. Our eyes met, and I saw the taunting bitterness behind his glazed eyes, smelling the beer and tobacco. I stiffened myself before this man, because he was such a network of mockery and frustration.

'You're a good fellow,' he said sentimentally. He looked at me mildly as though I were drunk and he had to make allowance. There were beads of sweat on his forehead. He became suddenly serious and wily. 'You're not one of us, are you? You haven't been here before? Ah, man, this is a cesspit, a place of lost souls. See that man of benevolence?' and he pointed straight at Thompson, who waved cheerily and burst out laughing. 'He's the spider, a human spider, that man. We are all damned, and that man feeds on us. He uses us as material for his short stories, his damned stories. Sucks out your soul and tosses you aside. . . . I only some because of the sandwiches, and because Catherine needs me. . . . Look at her pretending she can't hear what Paddy's saying! Isn't she beautiful? Ah, what a waste, what fragrance, beauty. . . .' He swayed back, and put a hand on my knee.

'Excuse me. Listen; I'm not drunk now – my mind's perfectly clear. You're an artist, aren't you? I can tell; you don't have to say anything. Sensitive, aware of things. Will you do me a favour? . . . Have a look at this . . .' He dragged a dirty sheet of paper from the inside pocket of his jacket. 'I wrote it last night. . . . Have a look at it. There you see that, The Keen. That's the title; it means a lament . . . a mother mourning for her dead son – read it. Bloody awful writing, I know. See what I mean? I can do things, can't I, when I get down to it? Not useless, am I? It's been in my pocket all this time and I've just remembered; that's why it's in a filthy state. Like me. Moving stuff, isn't it. Good? A mother, you see, keening. . . . .'

I tried to read his manuscript. It must have been about five hundred words, scrawled over the ruled foolscap. After I had read a few sentences I realized that I was unable to absorb it with people watching me, and gave it up, staring at the childish writing for a suitable length of time. Then I told him that it was good, putting as much conviction as I could into my voice. He lifted his head, and his dark hair fell over his face. I was afraid he would question me, but he only nodded sleepily, as though satisfied, stuffing the paper into a side pocket.

When Catherine got up to leave, it had turned midnight.

'Are you going to walk through the streets alone at this time of night?' asked Marjory in an anxious voice, and I grasped my opportunity.

'I'll come with you, shall I?' I said, getting up at once so that she could not refuse. I found my legs so weak that I had to scramble to my feet as Paddy had done, dragging myself up by holding the sides of the chair. It must have looked queer, but I was too tired to care what people thought.

We went for our coats together, with Marjory fussing round us. Paddy had fallen asleep, bunched in his chair, looking like a small boy who has eaten the wrong things.

'Looks as if we've got him for the night,' said Thompson thoughtfully. He stood in the doorway to the room, and pointed backwards with his pipe. 'This usually happens.'

Catherine had put on a neat blue coat, long and elegant-looking, trimmed with fur, and wore a sort of turban, yellow, to match the tiny stones of her earrings. Her face was like a sea-shell, very pale and velar, her eyes smiling curiously. Her expression seemed to be saying, 'It is all madness, extraordinary madness, this world.' But perhaps that was her tiredness.

'Good-bye, you two,' cried Marjory, singing out comfortably form the side of the house, and she leaned out a moment as we felt our way towards the gate. 'Don't dilly-dally!' And she closed the door.

We went on in silence for a long time, until it began to seem absurd. I kept trying to think of something natural that I could say. We could have been absolute strangers who had accidentally drawn level in the darkness, walking along side by side.

When we came to a crossroads I realized that I was lost, so I said, 'I hope you know the way. I'm just following you.' I had meant to be humorous, but I had spoken too softly, hushed by all the stillness. I thought of a desert that became a raging battlefield by day. The city night was strangely forlorn and sinister, yet beautiful too, with the beauty of the desert. Then a faint rain was falling, and I did not know it until I heard the stillness rustling all around us. Our feet rang out distinctly, echoing, as if we were in a vast hollow place.

'I know the way,' murmured the woman.

I glanced sideways at her face, very swiftly. It was burning white in the pools of dark, shining like a shell. She was gazing straight ahead and swinging her arms like a man.

We were walking at the edge of a long park, following the iron railings. On the other side of the railings it seemed dense with undergrowth and darkness, mysterious and secretive, like a jungle.

I suddenly turned to the woman at my side, almost loathing the silence which seemed such a mockery, containing nothing; but something in her face chilled me. It was set in an inscrutable expression, and I was baffled. I felt a flood of anger and humiliation; it was as if she were deliberately ignoring me. But I felt that she did not want me to remain so silent, that she wanted me to speak, to reveal myself. Her tenseness and expectation made my throat quiver and thicken; I was afraid to speak and have my voice break.

'Do tell me about yourself,' she said, as if to help me, her voice husky and low in her throat. Her face had changed subtly now, for there was something new and warm in it.

I laughed and looked away, trying to get my breath.

'You can be as frank as you like with me, you know,' she said, with a strange undertone to her voice. Her words flew into me like wasps, stinging me to speak.

'There isn't much to tell,' I got out at last, quite steadily. It was queer, unreal. I had listened to myself speaking as though my voice was disconnected from my body. Her words had disturbed and excited me, though I did not understand. What did she want to know? What could I tell her?

'Oh,' she said, and I could see that she resented what I had said. Yet I had not meant to snub her. She stared down as though bitterly at the pavement, and we strode on very quickly with barrenness between us. The air seemed electric. Looking at this strange woman, at her small mouth poised so precariously, about to grimace or cry or tighten coldly on itself, I understood how disappointed she was in everything, and how grimly she was prepared to be disappointed in me. It was all the same to her. Why shouldn't I disappoint her? Men were all alike. I was certain that this was what she was thinking, and I burned with rebellion and hurt pride, refusing to be confused with other men.

'Don't lump me with the others,' I said finding my own voice at last. 'You'll be wrong if you do.' I had clenched my hands in anger.

She lifted her head curiously, surprised. 'The others? What others?'

'The other men you've known,' I said, becoming confused at once, out of my depth. I had phrased it deliberately in a worldly way and it sounded stupid.

She laughed quickly, the sound ringing hard and bitter. But when she spoke again it was quite tenderly, as though she had a child to deal with.

'Do I do that? How do you know?' A faint smile of irony came to the corners of her mouth, yet I believe she was pleased. Her eyes shone with excitement, as if she felt something between us, below the words, and I grew more confident.

'I know,' I said.

'But how?'

I looked into her face without wavering, for the first time. We had both relaxed now and were ready to laugh. The air of tension had nearly gone.

'By your face,' I said, smiling. A little spasm of nervousness made me avert my own face.

'Oh dear, my poor give-away face,' came her voice. Then I blundered against her on the pavement. 'My fault,' she laughed. 'I should have told you to cross over here.'

We were climbing a hill near the Castle, and the clocks in the city began to chime their different versions of the first hour of Sunday morning. Lights were glowing in all the windows of the squat building that crowned the Rock, and I pointed to them.

'What are those lights, at this time of night?'

'Ghosts,' she said.

I looked at her, warmed by the gaiety of her voice, and found her face new and luminous, child-like, with bright, twinkling eyes. The mask-like effect still lingered, but its lines had broken and partly dispersed, and I saw that it was how she had deliberately applied her make-up, the red mouth burning on the startling whiteness, the eyes darkened and made tragic. Now it no longer frightened me, though I did not like it. I understood that it was something essential to her, this brittle elegance, like a shield.

There were no street-lights on the brow of the hill, and we entered a dark tunnel of trees. It was like stepping up to a solid wall which suddenly fell back, then rose up again, sealing us in. I thought of our bodies parting the darkness, like water dividing before the prow of a boat.

Almost shyly Catherine linked her arm through mine, as we trod forward blindly. Her touch was very light. I felt the tightness in my throat again and gulped for breath as noiselessly as I could.

I felt a wave of sickness and fatigue rising up in me, and tried to fight it away. We came out of the trees and now there were lights, and we moved down towards a crossroads in the hollow where a car had just swished past, the road falling away gently under my feet.

I felt extraordinarily light; my feet seemed to be just grazing against the pavement. Then I staggered and almost lost my balance, as we stepped into the road.

'I'm sorry,' I muttered, feeling dizzy and sick.

'Are you all right?' Catherine said, looking into my face.

'I don't know. I feel done in, all at once.'

'Why not sit down? Sit down here, on the kerb; it won't matter.'

We had reached the crossroads and had been half-way over. I crouched down obediently on the edge of the island in the middle of the road. Inside me everything was rocking and crumpling up. I felt ready to die.

'My God, what's the matter with us?' I heard Catherine say above my head. 'I feel weird myself, now.' And she sat down beside me.

We looked at each other out of pale faces silently. At last I gave a shaky laugh, feeling the sickness dying away.

I got up. There was somebody coming. 'Are you any better?' I asked, helping Catherine to her feet.

'I think so, but I still feel queer. Fancy the two of us being affected like that, together. What d'you think it was?'

She took my arm again and we went on, leaning on each other like two invalids.

'It didn't seem like anything physical,' I said. Then I burst out laughing.

'What's funny?' she asked, the wide, insatiable curiosity in her eyes again.

'I was thinking of Jack Kelvin. He'd say somebody was wishing evil on us.'

'Oh,' she said. 'And Marjory would say it was love had overcome us.'

'Is that the effect it has?' I laughed.

'I wouldn't know,' she said, with knowledge making her

eyes shrewd. I knew that I had said the wrong thing, that in another second or two she would retreat into elegance and assume the mask-like expression again, so I went on quickly:

'Do you know them very well at Thompson's – the others, I mean?'

She looked sharply at me. 'Not very well,' she said. Her expression went almost sinister with secrecy, and she shook her head. 'Well enough, though. I'm glad you came tonight, it needs some new blood there. Robert's quite nice, and Jim. I like Jim.'

'What does the foreign chap do for a living?' I asked out of curiosity.

'Kurz? He's a painter and decorator – wouldn't think it, would you? He's a displaced person, or something. God, he's a moody devil.' She stiffened her lips and made her mouth grim, glaring at me fiercely, as though challenging me to ask what she meant. It made me wonder what water I was getting into, so I changed the subject. Evidently there was a great deal I didn't know.

'How about Paddy – what does he do?' I was trying to imagine these strangers in their every-day lives.

Catherine averted her face, and when she spoke she put in all her disgust.

'He's a spiv of some kind – don't ask me what, exactly. All kinds of shady business, I think, drugs included. He takes them himself, some sort of other. You'll see him in mid-winter walking in the street wearing nothing but a short-sleeved cotton shirt and a pair of flannels, not feeling the cold because of the drugs he takes.'

She paused looking at me directly. 'Whenever he gets the chance he tries to paw me, the fool.'

There was nothing I could say, but I did not feel awkward. It was easier to be silent now, and I felt perfectly natural, walking with her, as if I had known her for a long time.

We had reached another crossing, where the road forked in three directions.

'This is where I live,' she said.

'Where?'

'That house on the corner. No, the other corner. You see the blue woodwork?'

'Oh yes.'

I stood foolishly, knowing it was a crucial moment, and she watched me, smiling with amusement.

'What is the number of your house, in case I should want to write to you?' I asked.

She told me. Then she raised her head, her eyes glinting with a dangerous light.

'Don't mind anything I say, will you?' she said. 'I can be frank, can't I? It won't shock you?'

'No, I don't mind,' I said.

She was not really bold, but she had gathered herself to say something. Now she suddenly jerked her head to look towards her house, and at the same time she said:

'I wanted you to come with me tonight. That was why I waited.'

I laughed with relief.

'I was hanging on for the same reason,' I said, and her

face glowed with happiness for a moment.

'I live with my father,' she said, 'or you could come in. I should like you to.' She looked at me frankly, smiling proudly, her eyes tinged with wistfulness. I stood like a fool. My desire would not let me speak.

'You like me then?' she whispered, though we still stood apart.

'Yes,' I said, and my heart seemed to swell, striking against my chest.

Then she did an amazing thing. Reaching forward, she bent her head, grasping my left hand and pressing it to her lips. She did it so swiftly that I hardly knew what had happened. Then she had darted across the road.

She stood on the corner for a moment, looking back, before going into the blue-painted house.

Chapter 16

I HAD begun to live for Saturdays. During the weekdays I worked conscientiously at the builder's office though nobody checked what I did. I enjoyed being careful and thorough, and I had learnt the way to make the time pass quickly was to become absorbed in whatever you were doing. It no longer mattered that the whole business of pay-sheets and income tax was meaningless to me; I had long ago become resigned to that.

When it was Saturday again, and time for Catherine to come, I found it hard to sit still. I stood in the room watching the buses as they rolled downhill under the window, sloping with oily smoothness into the heart of the city.

Kelvin was occupied at the table, writing a letter. Someone had shown him an advertisement in the personal column of the *Independant*: a girl who was a commercial artist invited correspondence from anyone, on any subject. She was bored to distraction with her job and would like something more 'creative'. But she was not afraid of any adventure, she would consider any proposal. All replies answered, etc.

Two or three times already he had set to work writing his letter, each time screwing the sheet up in despair and letting it drop on the floor. He was half-disgusted with himself, yet he liked the reckless note sounded in the advert; he was like that himself: ready for anything. He kept telling me that he could understand someone who felt like that. And someone had shown him the journal, so it was not his idea. Perhaps it was fate.

He laboured at another attempt now, his mouth snarling in his beard like an animal in a bush. Then he caught fire and was away, streaking over the paper, his words running into each other so that they were almost impossible to read. He came to the bottom of the sheet and cursed, turning the page over hastily, without raising his head. He always wrote his letters in a little book and kept a carbon copy. One day they might be valuable, he told me. He never lost his vision of ultimate fate.

It was gentle, early September weather. I watched the breeze lifting up the scraps of paper in the gutters, and felt the warmth of the mild sun through the glass. Kelvin had finished at last, and he sat back in triumph, throwing down his pen. I turned away from the window.

'What makes then "independant" anyway? Where did they get that name from?'

I was not really interested, but I had asked in order to start him talking.

'Ah, I don't know,' he said, rolling in his chair, with massive exasperation. He wrinkled his face. 'Expect she's just some silly art-student type out for a few thrills, when it comes to it. Yet it might be the real thing – who knows? You reckon it's genuine?' He had not even heard my question.

Before I could reply I heard Mrs. Perrin calling from the floor below. I went out on the landing.

'Visitors, Mr. Paul!' she shouted, her head flung back unnaturally. As she saw me come out, she jerked back into her room.

Afterwards I could not remember going downstairs, only

of being in the hall and walking forward with sedate steps.

Catherine and Jim stood in the hall, waiting for me. I was too surprised to be angry or disappointed. Then I became conscious of the shabbiness of everything, the worn linoleum, the blotchy, flaking distemper which flanked the stairway, the patches of damp, and a faintly squalid look about the stairs and landings which I had never noticed before.

Jim turned to me at the first landing, inquiring lazily if he had to go on up the next flight. His eyes looked mysterious now rather than sleepy, as if heavy with some secret knowledge. He wore a dark suit.

As we reached the door, Catherine hung back for a moment, letting Jim go in. Her face was gay with laughter and pleasure as I caught up with her. Behind Jim's back she put out her hand and touched my cheek. And for the next ten minutes my head was full of this.

I did have time to wonder what Kelvin's reaction would be. He had made up his mind not to approve of Catherine, and her companion would be a complete surprise, I thought. But he got to his feet cordially enough, slightly bashful, his ugly face flowering miraculously with a sweet charm. I introduced them both as well as I could, knowing that in a few moments he would be taking control of everything and steering the talk round to himself. It was what I wanted.

I took Catherine's coat into the bedroom, laying it carefully across my bed. It struck such a strange note in our bare room that I stood back and looked at it, lying there in neat lines on the faded eiderdown, the arms folded into the centre, crossing over.

Back in the other room, I found the atmosphere rather strained and subdued, with everybody talking in snatches, then falling into awkward silences. They all looked at me in relief as I came in. Kelvin could not really fathom Jim, who showed no response, no sign of life at all, just sitting there looking faintly amused, his face drowsy and heavy. Once again he reminded me of a reptile in baking heat. His whole body was inert, and I found it hard to imagine him walking about.

Catherine unwrapped a cylindrical parcel and held out a tin of apricots.

'Look!' she cried with vivid excitement. 'My contribution to the tea!'

'Oh yes,' I said, laughing. 'Thanks very much.'

'Take it, then, take it,' she cried, waving it at me.

'To tell you the truth,' I confessed, coming forward, 'I'd forgotten you were coming to tea.'

She looked at me with her wide-open eyes, and I stammered, 'I mean, I knew you were coming, but I forgot to get anything in.'

'Oh dear,' she said brightly. 'All right, then, *this* is the tea!' She made her announcement to the room and pointed at the tin of fruit in my hand.

We all laughed, and the peculiar air of tension left us. Jim brightened up, even asking a few questions, his eyes roaming lazily around the room. I saw that the pictures interested him, one or two especially, by the way his face became alert, his gaze sharpening. He started to tell us in a sleepy voice about a trip he had made to France with a friend a year ago, and how he had had to come back because his feet had blistered.

'We were going to hitch-hike to Provence,' he drawled, his gaze wandering, then resting on Catherine's face, where it stayed. 'The first night over there we slept on the station.' As he spoke a queer, voluptuous look swam into his face, under the skin, his lips opening a little. It struck me as something indecent, as though he were tasting some furtive thought before he uttered it.

'Go on,' said Catherine softly. Her face had gone quite ravenous with curiosity. I did not understand what was happening, but I wanted to break the spell of it.

'Talk about depravity,' Jim murmured, hardly moving his lips. 'God, Sartre couldn't hold a candle to it.' He made a splutter of embarrassed laughter from the back of his throat, shifting in his seat. He looked over at me suddenly and dowsed his voluptuous look. But I knew not what it was.

Kelvin gave a snort of irritation. The whole trend of the conversation seemed trivial and slack to him, so he began to inject his personality into it. It seemed the obvious solution. He started to talk about his favourite subject, which was himself.

The air became vigorous and healthy, frankly egotistic. There was much laughter and entertainment, with Kelvin impersonating people he hated, and things ran along easily. Then it was time for tea. I had sat perched on my chair, subdued and watchful, laughing with the rest, not offering much in the way of conversation. I liked to let it flow around me, listening; it was pleasant, though I attached no importance to it. 'Nothing of any importance can be said,' I thought. 'If it is vital and significant, it won't let itself be spoken. Words distort it. But life is not all vital significances. What is insignificant and trivial is sometimes very pleasant, very refreshing, if you can let it flow over you and know it for what it is. It saves you from too foolish an earnestness.' I must have looked like Kelvin's docile little monkey as I sat there, content to munch whatever was offered. 'Let life be a matter of picking up apples, wolfing the flesh and dropping the core . . . no more than that, sometimes,' I thought.

I went out to Mrs. Perrin's kitchen to boil some water and cut the sandwiches. Out of the corner of my eye I saw Catherine get up to follow me out, and hoped quickly that there would be no one else in the kitchen.

'I'll help you, Louis,' said Catherine, behind me, and I turned to look at her as if surprised. She was carrying the tin of apricots. The kitchen was empty. How beautiful she was now, I thought, as she rustled forward softly. I looked bashfully at her ash-blonde air, and at her body, at the lovely way it moved in the blue georgette frock.

'Let me slice the bread. Here, open this for me,' she said, taking charge of things. We stood shoulder to shoulder, childish and gay. Once our elbows collided as we stood there at the table with our heads bent forward.

I moved away to fill up the kettle and felt something strange. She had slipped something in my pocket.

'What's that?' I said.

'Never you mind,' she said, flourishing the breadknife in

my direction. 'Get on with your job. Look later.'

When I managed to look, I found it was a ticket for the circle at the Co-operative Theatre the following Tuesday evening. They were showing Berto Paskuas' Negro Ballet for two weeks. At the bottom of the rectangle of card she had written firmly in pencil: 'Meet you outside at seven?'

I carried in the food on a wooden tray, holding it gingerly because one of the handles was broken. Catherine followed me with a pot of tea, closing the door behind her. I saw Kelvin look at us with narrow wolf eyes.

'Lay the table, somebody,' commanded Catherine, and Kelvin got up without a word, setting to work.

'There ain't enough spoons,' he said as he ferreted in the sideboard drawer. 'Only tea-spoons.'

'They'll do, they'll do,' cried Catherine. 'Let's eat! by the way, who's giving this tea-party?'

She was happier than I had ever seen her. I wished I was alone with her, though I guessed that it was everything at this moment that was helping to make her happy. Even Jim's slumberous body, lumped at the table, made its contribution, and Kelvin's face, smitten with grudging wonder. There was a glow in the air around her.

Afterwards things took a different turn, and no one knew what to say. Even Kelvin seemed at a loss. He sat gazing down blankly, fidgeting with his cup. Catherine was clearing away, and when she came in again Jim had gone back to his armchair. He had taken the pornographic book with him, which had been on top of the sideboard, and he sat there in silence, flicking the pages. The stillness in the room seemed ominous, after Catherine had sat down. I wanted to look at her, but we were both refusing to do that. We only did it when the other looked away.

She sat facing Jim, one on either side of the fireplace.

'What have you got there,' she asked with gentle mockery.

I looked across then, as her words fell into the silence.

'You know,' said Jim. He spoke in a low voice, not looking up. 'That book I brought back from Paris.'

'Oh that,' she said. I saw the bold, modern look leap into her eyes, the glint of rapacious curiosity. It made me wince. She seemed as if hypnotized, her gaze fixed on the book he was fingering. I glanced quickly at Kelvin, but he was looking out of the window.

'Good Lord! what a book,' the man was murmuring. 'You ought to read this part.' His face had changed, and this time I understood. It was like something growing under a stone. He lifted his head and it seemed to float back on his neck like a bubble. He was gloating at Catherine, who sat very taut and still, her face pale.

'Want to see it?' he mocked. Then she gave stiff little smile and nodded, and he leaned out of his chair to hand it over.

I was glaring at the back of his head, full of an icy fury, feeling a deadly puritanical passion struggling up in me. I wanted to smash the book out of his hand. Yet I sat where I was and watched Catherine take the book from him, open at the page he had been gloating over. As she reached out, Kelvin turned his head to see what was happening.

She sat like a spring, keeping her fixed smile, crouching

over the book for a second or two. Then Kelvin broke into a short harsh laugh and her courage failed her.

'That's enough,' she said, laughing shakily, and handed the book back.

Until then I had felt nothing but rage and contempt. Now a shock of murderous hatred ran through me, a sort of delayed-action feeling. I had to fight hard to stop my hands from trembling visibly.

The rest of the evening was rather hazy to me. I kept brooding and plunging into orgies of hate inside myself, unable to concentrate on anything. It was as though I had let a devil loose. I was glad when our visitors had gone, so that I could come to grips with my chaos of emotions.

On Tuesday we sat in the theatre, and my blood was tingling with excitement even before the curtain lifted. We had fifteen minutes to wait, and I kept reading the exotic names on my programme: Momodu Kamara, Doris Bah, Mizeoden Boi, Berto Paskua. And I had forgotten until then what a sumptuous, pulsing world it must have been, the ancient theatre. I kept thinking of the old thunderers, the fanatical ravers, the splendours and miseries parading back and forth, the black tragedies and tremendous affirmations, the whole storming whirlwind of the drama.

There was a miserable fire-curtain which I hardly noticed.

I turned to Catherine, beautiful in her black dress with its ornaments of dull metal. How still she sat!

'It must be five years since I went to the theatre,' I told

her.

She smiled a secret smile, not answering, peering over the rail and scanning the stalls. It was alive with movement down there.

'You'll like this, I know you will,' she said. 'I wanted you to see it.'

She loved the bustle and excitement passionately, the charged atmosphere. She found it difficult to speak to me because of this. It made her sit perfectly still. It made her poise herself on her seat, warm and sensuous, like a cat. Her lips were shining, her whole body tense and erect.

The curtain rose, and the negro dance-drama came flooding out at us, enveloping us where we sat. The stage could not contain it; it was like a wave out of the sea. And it was in a frenzy through being baffled and pent up within civilization. Because of this contradiction, because it contained this paradox, it wore a grotesque, fanatical expression.

I had never seen anything like it before. I sat in a stupor, my senses wonderfully drugged, hearing the wild stomach shouts, the ceaseless tom-toms. Catherine was drumming on the boards with her right foot. She had forgotten about me. Once, at a moment of great intensity, she reached out and gripped my arm with fingers of steel.

I looked down at the dancers, at slack, effortless limbs, supple and duskily glamorous, at the snapping, glistening eyes in the vigorous animal skulls. The women were many-coloured, the men almost naked, their small round heads reduced to insignificance, all bobbing madly on the wild water of the music.

I did not know what to look at. Everything flowed without form, flooding about in an absence of struggle and barrier, orgiastic, with no gathering clouds of tragedy, no remorse, no memory. There were sudden earthquakes of catastrophe, eruptions, peaks of ecstasy flung up, moments of grief and pathos, but all without shadow or burden. It was like something rising through the grass and trees and animals, common to all. When disaster came it was swift and effortless, with no tragedy. You were struck swiftly over the heart with pity. Then everything was as before, with nothing changed, the blue sky dancing again with heat and innocence. Nothing was spoiled.

We sat watching it, spellbound. Neither of us could ever be like that again, though we felt we had once been those mindless dancers. We looked down on our old fathers. The beauty and majesty that we saw were artless, like the natural grace of animals. What we were looking at was the highest fruit of animal life.

'Look at the men, how narrow and straight they are,' breathed Catherine at my side, with intense admiration. 'I love their firm little buttocks, don't you? Look how they stand, how they hold themselves – oh, aren't they beautiful!' She gave me a wild despairing look, as if she could not bear the experience of it.

They were indeed beautiful. The men outshone the women; they inspired each other with greater and greater efforts, trying to become like gods.

Now she had eyes only for the leader, for Berto Pasuka.

He stood to one side, motionless, his arms hanging straight, like something planted to stand forever. He was full of dark power. There could be no mistake about him, he was clearly the leader, his head strangely intellectual and different. Thoughts burdened him. Authority sat between his brows, setting him apart. He carried the brand of it with pride. He would make brilliant knife-like movements that were authoritative. When he moved sometimes it was with a splendid languorous quality, like a naked man under water. And watching him come swiftly to rest, you thought of a steel spring coiling lean strength into itself, coil on coil, submerged in a thick oil. Then you held your breath, waiting for bonds to burst. This spring exploding was a magnificent sight.

A thin voice spoke complainingly from behind, almost into my ear.

'Rather sexy, isn't it?' said the woman.

Someone murmured agreement.

Catherine stiffened where she sat, darting a grimace at me, her face eloquent with indignation.

'You can't call it real ballet,' said the same voice.

And Catherine made the tiniest movement forward with her body, staring down at the stage with a tremendous concentration. She looked as if she were trying to reach the dancers below, to get some psychic message through the air to them. That was how it struck me. Then, as I thought this, I heard her hissing, 'Go on, go on! Hot it up! Shock them, go on!'

On the way back to her house she told me that she had met Pasuka, when his company had visited Nottingham once before. That had been her first taste of it, and it had overwhelmed her. She had gone backstage deliberately to meet him.

'He looked totally different in his clothes,' she said. 'Quite ordinary. I found him very reserved, hardly talking at all, though he speaks perfect English.'

It was nearly eleven when we reached her house. I slowed down unthinkingly as we came to the corner. We stood in the dark street. Some ancient instinct made me raise my head to the sky. It was full of soft light, the moon veiled by thin cloud. When I lowered my head again the darkness between the houses was like pitch.

Catherine said very quietly, 'I've got a confession to make.'

'Go on,' I said. My voice had become gentle of its own accord, a sort of night voice.

'There isn't any father. That was a lie I told you the other week.'

'Didn't you trust me?' I could hardly believe it. 'You weren't afraid of me?'

'No, not afraid. I don't know what, really. It doesn't matter now.'

We fell silent, looking anywhere but at each other.

'Will you come in?' she asked. She seemed to be struggling with herself.

'All right.'

'I want you to,' she said, smiling up into my face, and as

she did so she took my hand. We crossed the road in silence. About ten yards from the door of the house I felt my hand squeezed with firm pressure, and my knees went soft, my heart beating up in my ears.

Then we were inside the house. It was another world, too delicious to think about. While I knelt down and built a small fire, she ran upstairs to change her dress.

'It's rather a special one,' she explained, and now she wore a simple blue flannel blouse, tied loosely in a bow at the throat.

Little flames were clipping bravely at the dark hole of the chimney as I got to my feet. We faced each other, and then a painful shyness paralysed us both. I knew it was my fault; it had come from me first. Then it was touch and go, the evening falling to ruin about us, but this time I fought back with all my strength, refusing to let this paradise slip away.

'Show me your books,' I said with the last of my breath. 'I've never seen so many. What are those big ones?'

I sat blighted by my shyness, while she showed me her prized possessions. She realized that something was wrong, but she was helpless. After a time she grew angry and confused, imagining some humiliation. I saw the rich bloom of her mouth begin to harden and wither, and forced myself to act. She sat crouched on a stool, slightly below me. Like a blind man I hung down over her and kissed her, and she uttered a curious smothered cry of relief, twisting wildly and lifting up her arms to my neck.

It was a new joy for me. I sat with my arms around her, and she leaned back with her full weight against my legs.

We had let the darkness of the room gradually shape itself around us like an enormous bush. It had great secrecy and a little core of red fire.

'Did you live here with him?' I asked.

'Yes.' Her voice was startled. 'How did you know I had been married?'

'Thompson told me.'

The fire blazed up, making her cheek ruddy.

'There isn't much to tell,' she said in a small voice.

'Were you happy?'

She thought for a moment.

'He was very good to me. Too good.'

'Then you weren't happy?'

'No.'

I stroked her arms. We were at the front of the house, and the pavement ran against the wall of the room, under the window. But we heard no sound.

'Louis,' she whispered.

'Yes?'

'You're strange.' Her voice was very distant.

I laughed. I was too breathless to speak.

'You're not like other men.'

'I know.'

She was gazing into the flames.

'You don't say things, do you?' she murmured.

'Say things?'

She meant that I did not use words of endearment.

'No,' I said.

'Why don't you?'

'I don't know,' I said, with my heart heavy. 'I try, but they won't come out of my mouth. They stick in my throat.'

I thought I had offended her. She sat perfectly still. Then she said, 'I'm glad,' and turned to look at me. Suddenly I felt gloriously happy and grateful, and tears rose up in my eyes. I pressed my face into her hair, whispering, 'Take off your clothes.'

She had wide breasts, high up on her lovely white body. She gave me a look and my blood raced madly, and I knelt down in a daze of love and tenderness, putting my arms round her thighs. Then we lay down before the fire. Just at that moment we heard, slow heavy feet clumping past on the pavement. We laughed happily, touching each other, pinching and biting, rolling about, until our two passions fused and put an end to all playfulness.

We lay together drowsily on the floor of the room, the darkness swirling over us. It was like being at the bottom of the sea, in a muffled, sluggish world. The fire was nearly dead. I kept kissing the warm pulp of her mouth, touching her ripe breasts in a kind of wonder, that her body had fruited.

Later she grew cold and clung to me, curling herself up, making herself small like a child. She was silent for a long time. Then she told me something of her past life.

'I'm not your first woman, am I?' she asked wistfully, and then I told her about Stella.

'It was a failure,' I said. But I could not concentrate on it, my mind kept wandering away. The air was full of freedom and simplicity.

She fell silent, looking at me once with slow, contented

eyes.

'I think I understand,' she said.

The hours had been eaten away, and it was very late. I stood at the door, then turned back to her. It was hard to leave now.

'Don't go,' she said.

'I don't want to,' I said, not recognizing my own voice.

'Don't then. Stay here.'

Not knowing why, I shook my head.

'No, not here. We'll go away soon, won't we?'

My mouth was against her throat; I hardly knew what I said.

'Yes, soon,' she said, and I looked into her face. Her eyes were all soft with bloom.

I went back through the streets to the flat with my head full of mad thoughts.

Somehow the weeks passed, dragging, and we made our few preparations. Catherine had friends in London, so, to begin with, we were going there. We both wanted to be swallowed up in something big for a time, and it seemed the obvious place. But I didn't care where we went, and it was bound to be South. We had resolved that whenever we moved it would be 'South'. The very word seemed to evoke a different world from the one we had known. Perhaps we would go to Devon eventually and live there, but our plans were left vague deliberately. Catherine was anxious sometimes, but I did not want to decide too much. Something was brimming up in bright jets within me, fresh and strong, making me trust the future.

When the time came I gave in my week's notice. I had told Kelvin nothing of all this, knowing he would only condemn it. I made that inevitable by laughing away his advice. But he must have guessed what was happening, for he showed no surprise when I broke the news to him. And once, when I had been crawling into bed at three in the morning, I heard him mutter, 'You're a fool.'

It was a Tuesday evening in late November. We were leaving on the eight-thirty train the following morning.

There was a big, lively fire in the grate. I imagined the winter drawing slowly nearer and encircling the city. So far it had not entered the streets. The fire crackled and hissed. Kelvin sat writing page after page of lightning scribble to his *Indpendant* girl; I believe he was trying to arrange a meeting. For some reason of his own he was rather morose, but I had to tell him my news.

'I'm leaving tomorrow,' I said.

'Oh?' he kept his head down, and all surprise out of his voice.

'I'd better start packing my suitcase,' I said, and set to work.

He watched me when he thought I wasn't looking at him.

'Who with – the widow?' he asked at last, gruffly.

It sounded funny, and I laughed.

'Yes, the widow.'

He looked down at his letter and said nothing more.

The next morning I stood in the chilly room, ready to go. I had put my suitcase out on the landing. Kelvin was late, and sat at the table hurrying his breakfast, blinking his little eyes. One hand was lifting a spoonful of cornflakes as the other tilted the milk-jug above his tea.

I felt that in leaving him I was taking leave of the world of men for a while, and tried to have an appropriate emotion. But it did not seem very much to lose. Besides, I had to go. I wanted to prove myself as a man and a father.

Yet when I looked at him again, and in spite of this reasoning, I felt a stab of real regret. I thought suddenly that I had heard the last of his huge laughs.

'You're off, then,' he said.

I nodded.

He made no attempt to get up and shake hands.

'Ah well,' he said, in a flat voice. He looked directly at me, his eyes brightening. 'You don't do things by halves.'

Through the window the day was pink and grey. It seemed mild, but there was a wintriness folded into the sky.

'Good luck,' he said, bending forward to push food in his mouth, milk dripping from his spoon into the white dish.

I went through the door and closed it behind me. Then something made me open it again and poke my head into the room.

I'll remember you, and all this,' I said.

'Of course,' he mumbled, his eyes dreamy and wistful. He leaned on the table and looked at me.

'So long,' I said, shutting the door.

Then I set out.